Erich Schröder

The House

About Life and Love

Erich Schröder

The House

About Life and Love

A story that life wrote,
told by Erich Schröder,
thankfully dedicated to all the people
mentioned in this book.

Bibliografische Information der Deutschen Nationalbibliothek: Die Deutsche Nationalbibliothek verzeichnet diese Publikation in der Deutschen Nationalbibliografie; detaillierte bibliografische Daten sind im Internet über http://dnb.dnb.de abrufbar.

1. Auflage, © 2024 Dr. Erich Schröder

Herstellung und Verlag:
BoD – Books on Demand, Norderstedt

ISBN: 9 783758 325458

Preis: € 9,99

INHALT

A House Tells its Story

Luise closes the front door and the window. Then she goes to the stove and turns on the gas tap. She lies down on the bed and waits, hoping it will be quick. A few minutes later, there is a knock at the door. Luise stays in bed; she doesn't want to open. No one has knocked on the door of her shabby dwelling for a long time. But the knocking gets louder, then heavier and heavier. Luise sighs, then she gets up, turns off the gas and opens the door. It's Walter.

If Walter hadn't knocked on the door so forcefully at that moment, the house that this story is about would still exist, but not the story that follows. For Luise, Walter's unexpected visit was an intervention by God - and she never tried to take her own life again. Instead, she decided to build a house.

Yes, it's about a house, my old house. A house with a long and eventful history. It has seen very good and very bad times and many people who have filled this house with life with their stories. I was born in this house and have spent a large part of my life in it, the last 40 years together with my wife Cecilia, but more about that later. The house is much older than me. It was built in 1929 and I've been around since 1948, so I can only tell you about the first 19 years of the house from old documents, diaries and letters. But let's let the house itself (in another font) have its say and introduce itself first:

Many people think I'm beautiful, but most of them also think I'm a bit long in the tooth by now. In fact, I can hardly be described as immaculately beautiful: The outer skin of red bricks is already slightly weathered, the mortar between the bricks slowly crumbling, darkened over the years, but repaired in many places in a striking light gray. In the past, pigeons had been up to mischief here, probably hoping for access to a hiding place. The beautiful old front door made of brown-stained solid wood had warped over the decades and formed a finger-wide gap at the bottom. It was an entrance for cold air in winter and an ideal starting point for burglary tools of all kinds. A few years ago, the old door was replaced with a modern, brown metal door, which can supposedly withstand a burglar for a longer period. New, very heavy windows and a conspicuous alarm siren also make me look like a fortress against unwanted intruders. There is a story behind this, which we will come back to later.

The somewhat forbidding impression disappears as soon as you enter through the front door. Stepping into the high, spacious hallway with the old fireplace, you can feel the warm, cozy atmosphere of the house. Tuscan-style tiles, a display cabinet with old porcelain, a beautiful old crockery cupboard with a glass door and two large wood-framed mirrors reinforce the homely impression. Inside, all the doors are mostly open and provide a clear view through the living room to the large, glazed patio door and into the dining room and kitchen. The staircase made of light-colored solid wood leads to the upper floor. Here you will find the master's study, the housewife's realm, a small guest room and the bathroom. Behind a door is another staircase to the attic with a converted bedroom, another room and a large storage room, which is occasionally used for drying laundry. Above the two converted rooms is an attic that can only be reached via a ladder, a paradisiacal place for children where an adult can barely stand upright.

Hard Life in Troubled Times

But back to Luise, she was my great-aunt, the sister of my maternal grandmother, Mathilde. What does Luise have to do with the house? She had it built, she was the building owner. More about that later. Luise was clever, educated, strictly brought up and religious. To understand how this dramatic and almost fatal event came about, you need to know the background, which Luise wrote down almost in minute detail in her "Memoirs".

The year is 1926 and Luise is just 39 years old. Luise herself described the apartment in which the drama unfolded as a "hole" and her flatmates as "unpleasant". She had been living in this so-called knee-floor apartment halfway up the stairs for almost ten years. Even when she moved in, the walls of the apartment were wet, the chimney was leaking, as were the gas pipes. In the years after the First World War, it was very difficult even for a teacher to find an apartment at all in a large city like Düsseldorf, which had been partially destroyed. But the desolate housing situation was only the temporary climax of a long history of suffering. Luise had not had much joy in her life until then. And years before that fateful evening, she had occasionally thought about taking her own life.

Luise was born on August 23, 1887, the daughter of the Protestant pastor Friedrich and his wife Sophie. Luise's parents had six other children and two maids lived in the house regularly, so it was a very large household. Luise liked to retreat from the often-unpleasant reality into a fairytale world of witches and wizards, in which she believed. Such myths and legends were widespread in her Westerwald homeland. However, this gullibility often made Luise the target of ridicule from her classmates. Her performance at school was rather mediocre. Overall, she found the four years of primary school agonizing.

At the age of nine, Luise moved to Bochum to join the family of her paternal grandfather, the grammar schoolteacher Carl-Friedrich and his wife Elise Friederike Maria. Her grandmother's upbringing was strict and old-fashioned even by the standards of the time, e.g. in matters of dress, which earned Luise a lot of ridicule from her classmates. Her grades improved at secondary school, but her school years as a whole remained joyless and unhappy. In French of all subjects, one of her later subjects, she received her worst report card with a grade of 3-4. Her grandparents put this down to the children's dance school, where she received top marks. Torn between life with her strict grandparents in Bochum and her real home with her parents in Waldböckelheim, Luise no longer felt truly at home and accepted anywhere. As a result, she carefully sealed off her emotional world from her environment. When she finally graduated from the High School, she wanted to become a nurse. However, this wish was ignored and instead she was supposed to attend the teachers' college at her school. Given her great aversion to school of any kind, it was certainly not her inclination to become a teacher. Luise struggled through the three years at the college, although she hated the pressure of lessons and the cramming-filled days. She forced herself to do something of her own for at least a few hours in the evening, then she painted or wrote poetry. The homework for the seminar often dragged on until after midnight. This excessive demand led to a prolonged illness shortly before graduation. As a result, she lacked the necessary preparation time, so that in the end her exam was only enough to qualify her as a primary school teacher. She was physically weak and exhausted after the exam. Exactly why she then traveled to France remains unclear. Perhaps just to recover after the strenuous seminar? Or for additional language training? In any case, she went to the tiny town of Désandans, about halfway between Basel and Besançon. Her father's acquaintances, the pastor Charles and his family, lived there. Luise later described this time as the happiest of her life.

Charles Jr. of the same age, who studied theology and literature and taught her French literature, certainly contributed to this. With him, she was able to experience a tender, albeit brief and ultimately unfulfilled first love. Luise stayed in France for a year.

After passing her language exam in Münster and a brief intermezzo as a substitute teacher in Sobernheim/Nahe, Luise went to England in 1908. A couple who were friends initially took her to London. But the city showed the young trainee teacher its darkest and ugliest side. The accommodation assigned to her was extremely poor and she found the barracks atmosphere in the school very unpleasant. A transfer to another school in the north of England came in very handy but did not bring any significant improvement. The arrogance and disdain of the principal was particularly troublesome. At the end of her compulsory year, she had the opportunity to visit Edinburgh, Manchester and London again. Although she found the capital much more pleasant this time, her relationship with England had already become firmly established. In retrospect, she felt that year in England was the worst time of her life. This was followed by a year at home in Bochum on her grandfather's orders to learn housekeeping and nursing.

After several unsuccessful applications, Luise finally found a job as a teacher in Offenbach/ Main. However, her time in Offenbach came to an end after just one and a half years when she complained of depression after her room was broken into. A short time later, her school was closed. Shortly afterwards, Luise received an offer to teach at elementary school in Düsseldorf. In the years that followed, she was frequently employed at different schools. At first, she lived with a cousin of her father. When her younger sister Mathilde also moved to Düsseldorf to complete a commercial apprenticeship, the two of them found a small apartment together. Luise met Walter Balthasar Corde, a talented but little-known painter from the Düsseldorf School of Painting, at a joint party at the Malkasten artists' pub. During a visit to his large but shabby studio, she was fascinated by his works and fell in love with him. Then the First World War broke out. Walter was drafted.

Everything changed for Luise too. At the beginning of the war, school buildings were requisitioned for military purposes and women were conscripted into the medical service or the military administration. But it was very difficult to get to the places where they were needed, because every journey was very strenuous. Cars did not yet exist; all trains were reserved for troop transports and shipping on the Rhine was also partially prohibited. The journey to Bad Kreuznach alone took many days under the most difficult conditions. Despite these obstacles, school soon resumed in Düsseldorf. Mathilde was back in Waldböckelheim, and so Luise temporarily lived with her sister Frieda, who was also a substitute teacher in Düsseldorf. But the war increasingly determined everyday life in the town. Apartments and rooms became increasingly scarce, so Luise had to move several times because the landlords needed the space. The rooms were usually sparse and shabby. But they had to be accepted as they were, because tenant protection or tenants' rights were still unknown. The walls were often damp, and in the very cold winter months, wood or coal for heating became increasingly scarce. Schools were also affected, meaning that children, who were already malnourished, were often ill. Food was hard to come by and, like everyone else, Luise suffered from hunger. She often only ate turnips when they were available. Luise's body deteriorated, she became depressed and her overstimulated nerves occasionally produced hallucinations. On top of this came constant, agonizing headaches. The last move in the war year 1917 was to the room that Luise herself described as a "hole", as already mentioned.

The poor living conditions did not initially change significantly when the war ended in 1918 and Düsseldorf came under Belgian occupation. In addition, there was a rapid and catastrophic devaluation of money, which eventually led to a currency reform "one billion to one". Shortly before the money became completely worthless, Luise managed to buy a piano. But in the end, the physical and nervous breakdown made her so ill that she had to take a leave of absence from teaching, first for six months and then for a whole year. She spent this time on recuperative trips to southern and eastern Germany.

In the turmoil of the war that had just been lost, another, no less significant event received far less attention: the second and deadlier wave of Spanish Flu, which raged worldwide from 1918-1920, now also reached Germany. It hit the exhausted country in a situation that could hardly have been more unfavorable. In total, an estimated 50 million people died worldwide, far more than because of the war that was raging at the same time. Luise's father Friedrich was also affected by the severe infectious disease, as he himself recorded in his diary (in the original wording):

"That I had greatly declined physically during the war, I have told. Now the Spanish Flu was sweeping through the country and claiming an incredible number of victims. I also fell ill but hoped to be able to keep going for as long as possible. When I couldn't go on any longer, I wanted to try another change of scenery until confirmation had taken place that year. So, I traveled to Enkirch with Hilde and Margarete. I had hardly been there a few days when I suddenly realized that I had a pleura and where it was sitting. It was high time. We took the next train home. There was no connection in Bingerbrück for four hours. I felt I couldn't wait any longer. So, I walked to Langenlohnsheim. Most of the luggage had to be carried by my two daughters. I was only able to take a small amount on myself. In Langenlohnsheim we got on the electric train and traveled to Kreuznach, where we just managed to catch the train of the small railroad that took us to Brauchemühle. Fortunately, we met Jakob Trapp and Georg Kiltz there with a wagon. I climbed up, but then my strength failed me. I fell backwards but was grabbed by the two gentlemen at the last moment and lifted back onto the cart. At home in bed, I immediately sank unsteadily into ever greater depths.

Pleurisy, the doctor explained. After a few days, the illness seemed to be over. My birthday came. It was my

60th. The Münchs came to visit. Mrs. Bertha wanted to do me a favour and sang the 53rd chapter of Isaiah from Handel's Messiah: "Truly he bore our sickness, the man of sorrows, full of wailing and anguish." She sang it beautifully, but every note went through me. When I got back into bed, I felt a raging pain, as if someone was piercing my lungs with red-hot daggers. Pneumonia, the doctor explained. I wrestled with death for weeks. And my loved ones fought with me. My dear wife and my daughter Hilde in particular did everything humanly possible to care for me. And my sister Martha faithfully stood by their side. Dr. Mießen also checked on me twice a day. Nevertheless, it is a true miracle of God that I pulled through. One night my pulse had already stopped. A cup of the heaviest coffee got it going again. I had to give up work for five months. I only interrupted this break once to perform the confirmation of the confirmands. Without exception, the congregation had the impression that this was my last official act. Through God's goodness, my spirits gradually revived. I was able to go to Wiesbaden for 3 weeks. When I left, I was able to walk 1 km with difficulty. When I came back, I had walked for miles and hours through the wonderful Wiesbaden woods. On the second day after my return, I met our doctor again on my bike. He came up to me with his stick held high. "It's just to try it out," was my reply. But it went well. Most of those who fell ill with rib and lung inflammation in those days after the Spanish Flu had to die from it."

Walter had returned from the war unharmed and had resumed his painting. He wrote back to Luise, and after a grace period, she agreed to visit him in his studio. She was again fascinated by his art and fell in love with him all over again. They grew closer, but the relationship was difficult, a rollercoaster between escape and rapprochement. Walter was a brilliant and hard-working artist, but a miserable businessman. He received large commissions that took him months of work to complete, only to have them taken out of his hands by others. He was unable to properly assess the value of his work and often sold his works at ridiculously low prices. As a result, he lived very simply and rarely had enough to eat. There were often arguments with Luise about this. It was also during this time that Walter saved Luise's life by knocking on her door unexpectedly. After that, he regularly spent a lot of time with her on long walks, which stabilized her condition again. But now it was time to change something in her life.

A Dramatic Birth

There was also news in Luise's old home - and it was no less dramatic. In 1914, her sister Mathilde became engaged to the merchant Erich Overhoff from Enkirch/Moselle. He was initially drafted into the medical service in 1915, but then volunteered to go to the front as an officer. On the Eastern Front, where he earned medals for some heroic deeds, he fell ill with rheumatic fever and was brought home for a lengthy stay in hospital. After several months in a field hospital, he was transferred to a clinic in Kreuznach and was thus back in his home country. On July 25, Mathilde and Erich married in Waldböckelheim. Erich had to return to the front in September 1916, this time in the West. After many long battles on various parts of the front, he was granted special leave to attend the birth of his child. However, due to an unforeseen turn of events in the war, he never reached home. Erich Overhoff was killed in action in Belgium on May 2, 1917, just ten days before the birth of his daughter Erika. His body was repatriated and arrived in Enkirch on May 12, 1917, exactly on the day Erika, my mother, was born at 12 noon.

It is said to have been a difficult birth, which is not surprising under the circumstances. Mother and child only survived with a lot of luck. Perhaps little Erika's heart was damaged in the process, which was later to be her undoing. Medical care during the war was certainly very limited. Mathilde returned to her parents in Waldböckelheim. Erika was a small, petite girl. She went to school there, for secondary school she had to travel 15 kilometers by bus to Bad Kreuznach. But in winter on the snow-covered mountain roads, it was unhealthy and dangerous. The bus had broken windows and no heating, and once it slid down a slope in icy conditions. Fortunately, Erika was unhurt. This went on for a year until everything suddenly changed.

A Courageous Plan Succeeds

Luise endured living in her "hole" for a total of twelve years. Then, when she had recovered somewhat from her short-sighted act, she had finally had enough. In addition, her father, who had just retired at the age of 70, had expressed an interest in moving to Düsseldorf with his wife, Mathilde and Erika. A larger and tidier apartment was needed. But such a rented apartment was hard to come by at the time. It was a good thing for Luise that the "hole" had one decisive advantage in addition to all the misery: the monthly rent of 27 M was very low. This enabled her to save 5,000 M in the years after the currency reform. This was enough to buy a plot of land in the north of Düsseldorf. She now wanted to build her own house on this plot. As the additional costs had to be financed by a mortgage, the overall budget was limited. A detached house was therefore out of the question. In the end, Luise ordered a terraced end house in a group of three houses through the economic office for trade and commerce. This laid the foundation stone for the house. It cost a total of 40,000 M including the plot, plus a few special requests, further purchases and the move. The move alone was to cost 1,000 M. However, when it came to moving in, the removal man demanded double that amount and immediate cash payment, otherwise he would take the piano away again. Only with the help of a strong neighbor was Luise able to convince him to keep the original price.

And now I, the house, come into the picture and will have my say from now on! As soon as I've finished, I'm standing here in the middle of a bare building plot, on which topsoil has been piled up but no plants are yet to be seen. My interiors are just as bare and still look quite uninhabitable. But that should change soon, the first furniture and the piano are already here. And the first preparations are also underway on the property. Fruit and vegetables are to be harvested here as soon as possible; a chicken enclosure is also planned. And the owner is said to have a weakness for roses.

It was a very brave decision on Luise's part to commission me, the house. For one thing, it pushed her to the limits of her financial resources. Her changing jobs offered no guarantee of a permanent, reliable income, which was necessary to service the mortgage. Luise was taking a risk here ~ a decision made out of necessity, but also out of a deeply felt responsibility for her family. On the other hand, the construction industry, which was flourishing again, had a harsh tone that certainly did not always make it easy for a young woman. The example of the freight forwarder shows this impressively.

During the move in 1929 and the first few days in the new house, Luise was supported by her sister Mathilde. The first night in their own house was rather scary for the two sisters, especially as they had heard of numerous break-ins in the remote suburbs of Düsseldorf. When a cardboard box in front of an open window in the cellar was knocked over by the storm with a loud bang, the shock was great and the first night was sleepless.

Then 12-year-old Erika moved in with Luise in the new house and lived with her for a year. This enabled her to continue her secondary education in Düsseldorf and the problem of the bus journey to Bad Kreuznach was a thing of the past. In May 1930, Luise's parents Friedrich and Sophie and her sister Mathilde also moved into the new house. The furniture arrived in two shipments from Waldböckelheim and Enkirch. For the first time since she had moved in with her grandparents at the age of nine, Luise lived with her immediate family again.

Now my still new walls were filling with life, after all, three generations of the family were already represented here. The old pastor Friedrich, probably still wistfully remembering his pretty vicarage in Waldböckelheim, described his new home, i.e. me and my condition at the time, in his diary as follows:

"The house is nice, well practical, shall we say. Solidly built, surrounded on three sides by the garden and only adjoining the neighboring house on one side. On the ground floor two rooms and the kitchen, on the second floor the two rooms that have become our retirement home, the bathroom and a small room, the so-called library room, in which I am writing these lines. Finally, under the roof, two small rooms, one the bedroom of my Luise, the other that of my Hilde and Erika. When we moved in, the garden around the house was still barren, like a barely cleared building site. Now (a few years later) it is full of trees and, as far as they still leave room, flowers of all kinds. An arbor that I built is covered with Waldböckelheim ampelopsis and Boos wisteria. Five apple trees, two pear trees and four peaches give hope for future fruit. Two beautiful cherry trees had to be removed again because they had no other purpose than to fatten up blackbirds. And then the stately walnut tree, Luise's favorite! The shrubbery in the front garden, also of Waldböckelheim origin, enjoys only very mixed popularity. Numerous berries have already aroused unanimous enthusiasm due to their regular good yield."

Art, Literature and a Tragic End

Luise was a great connoisseur and lover of classical German, French and English literature. She was particularly fond of Shakespeare. She had a large library in her study with the relevant works, most of which she probably read. But not only that, but she was also extremely active as a writer. She typed texts and stage directions for numerous plays on her old, naturally manual Remington typewriter. These included comedies, but above all dramas that were strongly oriented towards classical literature. In addition, she later wrote a remarkable three-volume war diary, which is an important documentation of the family's life during the Second World War.

Her artistic spirit was a kindred spirit with that of her friend, the painter Walter Corde. The two were in love and friends, but probably not a couple. One reason for this may have been the age difference; after all, Walter was eleven years older. Religion may also have been an obstacle, as the Catholic painter and the Protestant pastor's daughter would have had problems with a church wedding at the time. Some of the painter's pictures and sketches still adorn the house today. In particular, the monumental painting of the back of a cow dominated the stairwell for years. Fortunately, at some point much later, an enthusiastic buyer was found for the painting.

In the end, Walter was marked by cancer and increasing deterioration. In hospital, after a temporary separation due to misunderstandings, he and Luise had their last loving encounters and reconciliation. For both of them, Walter's last days provided space and time for a peaceful but also painful farewell. Walter Corde died on October 8, 1944; Luise remained unmarried.

The organization of the family's life together within my walls worked well. Mathilde ran the household. Luise provided for the family income with her lessons, now in a private school, together with the old pastor's pension. Erika was a good pupil and dreamed of studying chemistry. She completed grammar school up to the Abitur, which she passed with "good". And the two old people enjoyed living together as a family. But little did they know that the family idyll was about to be put to the test. The political skies over Germany darkened again, war polemics increased, and the Second World War loomed on the horizon. It was also going to get uncomfortable for me ~ and quite crowded.

New Politics and War Ideas

The fateful year of 1933 ushered in a new era in German politics, the effects of which were initially barely noticed. On the contrary, the successes of the new rulers were initially cheered. Things were moving in Germany, unemployment was reduced, the infrastructure was improved, allies were gained, and border issues were newly regulated. As a teacher, Luise had little choice but to join the ruling NSDAP party. Like almost all young people, Erika was also obliged to join the political youth organizations. But Luise felt the new tone in the country through unjustified transfers to other schools and the increasing rebelliousness of an indoctrinated youth. The old pastor Friedrich also thought less and less of the ruling party, whose hostility towards the church was becoming increasingly apparent. However, he himself was spared calls to join the party. On August 19, 1936, Friedrich and Sophie celebrated their golden wedding anniversary in a family atmosphere in their own home.

The non-aggression pact with Russia on August 23, 1939, came unexpectedly and gave rise to the first doubts about the seriousness of the rulers' assurances of peace. And then, on September 1, 1939, at 4.50 a.m., the Second World War began in Poland.

House and Residents Defy the War

No one of my generation, who has experienced nothing but the 79 years of peace in Germany so far, can really imagine what it means in concrete terms when whole squadrons of enemy planes appear in the sky to drop bombs on the city. When the sirens wail, you only have a few minutes to open the windows so that they don't shatter in the blast and then hurry to the cellar. But even there you are not safe. In the event of a direct hit, the house would collapse on top of you - and you had to be always prepared for that in the event of an alarm. How grueling it must be when the attacks occur daily, often several times a day, for years with no end in sight! No night allows for undisturbed sleep, and every trip outside, to work or to get food is associated with immediate danger to life outside the shelters. Today, images of the destruction caused by such attacks are only seen on television from current theaters of war. But experiencing this at first hand is a completely different dimension of horror. Luise's unvarnished, realistic diaries from the war years allow us to experience the brutality of everyday life at the time, with all its destruction, pain, hunger and despair. The daily walk to work, past the fresh, still smoking rubble of entire streets, the constant repairs to the house, the lack of food and the small amount of luck when she managed to get hold of something to eat - all this made fear and horror a constant companion of everyday life.

Luise describes her 56th birthday on August 23, 1943, in her war diary in her own words:

"We couldn't have started celebrating my birthday today any earlier and not under stranger conditions. Shortly after midnight the siren sounded the alarm. Then it was dead quiet for a long time. Only Schöller's shining window disturbed me. I rolled over and tried to go back to sleep and fell into a doze. But then it seemed to me as if heavy bombers were flying in. But as no one was firing and there was no headlight to be seen, I thought it was our returnees. But Schöller's light was still not dimmed. I called out to Hilde. Erika replied angrily and sleepily: "Why don't you go over and tell them?" I got dressed. Meanwhile, the incoming bombers sounded more like an enemy formation, and Hilde got dressed too. In the meantime, Dad shouted with a bard's roar: "Lights out!" And the light over there went out. Still no shots were fired. The muffled roll of the bombers continued over the clouds. We met in the cellar and said: "Now it's time for the little one to get up. It's bad where they fly up there." Then a shooting started in the south. Hilde fetched Erika, who in the meantime had also thought the situation was precarious. One chair was still missing. I fetched it down. But as soon as it was in the air-raid shelter, a thundering of airplanes came over us. The small airport cannon barked; the large anti-aircraft gun was missing. And then it roars... We cover our ears, hold our breath in suspense... wow... it has fallen. The tin lid on the cellar window pops up. And: wham, wham, wham, it goes outside. Now we're all standing on the inside of the room, because at any moment the window entrance could be blown open by dust. Then it comes down with larger calibers and the high-pitched whistling "ssssiu". Involuntarily, everyone opens their mouths and puts their hands over their heads. Then something hits nearby. Upstairs in the house there's a crash, walls shake. I run to the main gas tap and close it, then to the iron security door, and everyone prepares to flee. I can see through the window of the workroom that there's a fire somewhere in Düsseldorf. The sky is bright red. Hilde turns on the water cranes in the laundry room. Erika wants to go upstairs. But halfway up the stairs she falls back: boom, siiiu, boom, boom, boom, there's a crash all around. Then suddenly there's a great flare of ammunition above us. "They've got one!" everyone shouts. But nobody goes to see the spectacle this time. The tin lid over the cellar window dances like a madman through the air suction and air pressure. The walls and doors shake in concert. Then came the heavy near-impacts. "Silence! As long as you can hear the bomb, it's not immediately dangerous". One of the Smidts over there shouts: "Now it's time to open the wall breakthrough!" A stone is knocked out. Meanwhile, Hilde has run up to the first floor to see if we've been hit. "There's a fire at Schöller's," she shouts. Erika runs after her: "There's a fire at our place too!" she shouts. Theo rushes upstairs. We pass the news on to Smidts. "Then it's better to put the stone back in the opening," shouts Theda, "otherwise the draught will feed the fire." We search for the stone in the dark. Finally, the three come from above with a candle. "There's no point helping now. The firebomb fell next to our terrace. It was blazing, but it's out." It looked like rooms were on fire.

In contrast, flames were shooting out of Schöller's roof. The front cellar was as bright as day. From time to time, someone would run up and try to get over. Perhaps the Schöllers were unaware of the danger in their heavily concreted air-raid shelter. But the bombers were still circling close above us. Everyone had a watch in their hand. The attack time had to end every minute. Finally, there was a pause. A shrill fire engine whistle blew a storm in front of Schöller's house. I ran over and asked how we could help. "We need a spray pump and buckets of water." "Should we clear it?" "No, it needs to be put out," came a voice from upstairs. I ran back. Flak fragments were still raining down. "I'll bring the sprayer," Hilde called. "Hold on to the buckets so we can get them back!" I take the buckets, fill them at the barrel and run into the neighbor's house. The carpets are still there. But Mr. Schöller is standing at the source of the fire, pumping from full buckets. I refill mine. The ceiling comes loose and debris with glowing ash pours over me. Pouring the last bucket of water into the embers and then running out again is a matter of seconds. "We need buckets!" they shout from the cellar. I press mine into their hands and run out onto our terrace to get the hose. - In the meantime, the planes had gone. It was extinct up in the air. Instead, there was all the more funfair on the street. People from the neighboring houses and streets ran over, partly to help, partly just to look. Soon there was an overflow of people in Schöller's house. So, I persisted with my attempt to screw on the hose. It didn't work until Theo helped me. Then I tried to spray our house wall wet in case the fire jumped over. But the water pressure was so weak that it didn't reach the second floor. In between, Hilde came over: "Where's Erika?" I dropped the weakly leaking hose into the tub so that at least it would be full again and told mother to turn it off if the barrel was full again. Looking for Erika in the dark was difficult. She wasn't among the people at Schöller's. After all, someone had seen her in the neighboring street with Ursel Eichler rescuing furniture from a hopelessly burning house. Someone else knew that she had come back and was in Schöller's house. I looked for her but couldn't find her. Meanwhile, one roof section after another was collapsing. Where was the girl! Mother claimed that Theo was in Schöller's house with her. "More water! Our water is failing!" she shouted from inside. A strange woman pressed two buckets into my hand. I wanted to fill them at our tub. The water came pouring down the garden path towards me. Mother had forgotten to close the crane and the full water pressure had now returned. I jumped through the house, reached the barrel from the back and turned off the crane. We went back and forth like this for a while. Eventually, everyone gathered in the kitchen, soaking wet and hungry. "Congratulations on your birthday!" they jeered at me. Then we ate breakfast. "I want to see what our roof looks like," I thought and went up the dark stairs - because the light wasn't working yet. But then I stood in the bright moonlight in the attic and the fallen mortar crunched under my feet. Well, nothing more than slipped bricks! In the morning, Erika covered it up again on her own and put it back in place. Downstairs, Theo discovered that a large piece of ceiling had fallen down in his room. We didn't have to complain about a lack of dirt in the house. In the meantime, they had mastered the fire over there. We went to bed when five o'clock struck and one of us wished the others "Good night!" - once ironically, but then also with the relieving feeling that death had passed once again. There was a lot of noise in the house next door. The landlord must have lost his nerve somehow. He had already belittled Theo, the brother-in-law, when he intervened to help. But that didn't matter. We were just dead tired, and the rising sun saw only sleeping people in the mud, rubble and dirt. In the morning, of course, there was a lot of toing and froing until the family gathered in the provisionally cleaned house around midday. Preserved asparagus and butter sauce, some sliced veal and potatoes were the birthday feast. In the meantime, while shopping, I had learned that the attack had targeted all the suburbs of Düsseldorf: farmhouses, settlers' huts and the deaconess institution were on fire. The radio said: "Minor property damage."

It was not only a hard time for the people, but also for a house! Even my strong outer walls trembled under the detonations and pressure waves. My weak points, windows and roof tiles, were repeatedly damaged and then had to be repaired quickly to prevent the rain from penetrating. It wasn't always easy to get hold of the materials needed for the repairs. My housemates had to do the work themselves anyway. Fortunately, I didn't get a direct hit, otherwise my story would have ended right there.

Science and Love in Times of War

From today's perspective, it seems hard to imagine, almost impossible, to complete a difficult scientific course of study at the beginning of the war, which was to become a world war - and to fall in love at the same time. Erika managed the seemingly impossible and studied chemistry in Leipzig and Bonn. Erika herself describes how chaotic conditions were during her studies in a letter dated April 13, 1944, in which she talks about exam dates with various professors:

"I am very tired. I've been in Bonn since the day before yesterday and I'm having the big run around here. I've finished everything at the business office. Then I ran around appointments. I must have been to each one 5-6 times. Finally, Pfeiffer was scheduled for today at 11 am. Yesterday evening at 8 o'clock I was told that I had to go to Schulemann today at 10 o'clock. Since I didn't want to do that until Saturday, I had to study last night. Of course, the average sleep time at night is currently 4 hours. So, I went to Schulemann. When I got to chemistry, I was told that Dilthey wanted to test at 11 o'clock. Pfeiffer was at 11 o'clock. He fluctuated between good and very good. So Dilthey came in the afternoon. The alarm was sounded until 4 o'clock. At 5:30, despite the pre-alarm, Dilthey was there and only tested dyes. He said it was quite good. Censorship is still pending."

Another letter from Erika dated March 1, 1944, 6 weeks before the exams, tells us what the exam preparation was like:

"After 8 days of running around, I moved out of my stalactite cave with a killer cold and am currently staying with Schiefgens. Now I'm home to do some science. Can I visit you at Whitsun, or should I go to the Moselle if you can't use me? Time is pressing before then. I still have some running around to do, firstly about the bomb damage and secondly about my exam papers. But it will probably be done by Whitsun. If Tommy (nickname for English soldiers) keeps his bombs to himself. Only two canisters landed in our house. The fire department arrived in half an hour with two fire engines, but it still burned for 24 hours. The kitchen collapsed. Two apartments above and the roof are as good as gone. Heavy work is already underway. The pile of rubble is almost as high as the roof. What surprised me most was how much water two hoses can throw into a house in 24 hours. You wouldn't think it possible."

Erika got to know and appreciate her fellow student Hermann-Josef Schröder during their joint scientific work. Hermann-Josef had been drafted to the Eastern Front in Russia in the meantime but was discharged home due to a serious illness. The two became a couple. In 1944, the year of the war, they both completed their chemistry studies with top marks and obtained their doctorates - an extraordinary and almost unbelievable achievement under the circumstances, which deserves respect and recognition! There is a short but very meaningful letter from Erika to Luise about their wedding on November 4, 1944:

"Now I am married. We made our honeymoon journey by bike from Bonn through the ruins of Cologne to Düsseldorf. I'm dead tired. Grandpa will marry us the day after tomorrow."

Pastor Friedrich describes the wedding at home, also in a letter to Luise, who was unable to attend the wedding, as follows:

"On November 2, 1944, the bride and groom arrived at our home. The civil wedding had already taken place on October 28. It was decided that I would perform the church ceremony in our house on November 4, 1944.

At around 10 o'clock on the evening of November 2, we experienced the heaviest Tommy attack ever in our Düsseldorf suburb. The floor of the cellar shook and trembled under the impact of enemy bombs and shells. And - let's just admit it - our hearts also trembled as often as the explosions took place in the immediate vicinity of our house. As was to be expected, our house and the entire neighborhood up to the road to the airport suffered severe damage. Our house had 350 roof tiles destroyed, so that the rain pouring down at the same time had free and damaging access to the interior of the house. 19 of the large windowpanes were broken, several doors, including the beautiful front door, were damaged and no longer closed. The door to our bedroom was completely shattered. During the night, my wife, Hilde and Erika did their best to remove as much mud as possible from the floorboards.

November 3rd had to be devoted exclusively to preparations for the wedding. This included removing the broken tiles from the roof. Some of the remaining tiles were used to make a makeshift covering for the western half of the roof. The remaining unbroken tiles were used to cover the eastern half as far as the two attic storeys of the attic. This work was carried out by the young couple under almost uninterrupted rain, as no other forces were available, and they even had to spend a few hours of the wedding day on it. In this way they at least managed to get a rain-free room for the wedding night. The considerable preparations for the wedding feast were of course in the hands of the bride's mother and grandmother. It was certainly no easy matter to organize even a simple wedding feast under the prevailing conditions of the world war. Fortunately, my eldest daughter had been able to bring a jar of roast venison with her on her last visit. The Wermes family also provided a number of good gifts for the wedding day. My task was to conduct the necessary negotiations with the church authorities and to prepare the wedding sermon.

The ceremony itself took place on the 4th of this month at 12 noon. The neighbors had gone above and beyond to provide the necessary floral decorations for the altar table, making it possible to decorate the wedding room beautifully. Hilde accompanied the chorales on the piano. The spiritual song "Harre meine Seele" opened the ceremony. For the wedding text I had chosen the saying: 1 John III verse I: "Behold, what manner of love the Father has shown us, that we should be called children of God." This was the bride's confirmation verse. The song "Ach bleib mit Deiner Gnade" led to the wedding vows and the final prayer and blessing. The ceremony ended with the song "Praise the Lord, the Mighty King".

Unfortunately, the ceremony had to be held within the immediate family circle. The bride's mother's and mother-in-law's sisters and sisters-in-law were invited, but too late to attend. The groom's parents were also unable to attend due to the great difficulties of the journey."

The War Comes to an End - Misery Remains

In March 1945, enemy ground troops began the siege and capture of the city of Düsseldorf. Even the precautionary demolition of Düsseldorf's three Rhine bridges could not stop them. Many private houses were confiscated. This continued until Berlin was also taken in May 1945. An armistice was finally signed on May 9, 1945. There were no more attacks, but the situation remained bad for the time being. The German state collapsed. The dreaded consequences: Salaries were no longer paid, civil servants became unemployed, the banks stopped issuing money, the post office remained closed. The food situation was already very bad. The general ration was one pound of bread per week, 300 grams of meat, nothing else. No fat, no nutrients, salt had been missing for 4 months, sugar for longer. And coal was scarce and would be missing in winter.

Luise now earned her money by giving private lessons. Demand was high. Many parents were afraid that their children would no longer be able to go to school and were mainly looking for English lessons - probably with an eye on the occupying forces. Luise did not have a large income, but at least she had a regular one.

In an epilogue to her war diary, Luise writes:
"The worst was over. At least no more people were killed. As terrible as the post-war years became, the long period of hunger, the hunt for the most essential bread, with excessive hauling of turnips, among other things, the lack of coal in a very harsh winter, the cramped conditions in the apartments (7-8 of us sat in the kitchen all day), the dangerous and exciting journeys on coal wagons, Erika even when she was 7 months pregnant with Gerd, the escape with the furniture at night and in the fog when there was a risk of squatting, etc., none of this outweighed the horrors of the Nazi government with its unbearable compulsion of conscience, dishonesty and hopeless prospects...
So, I couldn't help feeling happy when we finally lost the war. The end, the end! It was over."

Farewells and New Life

On October 18, 1945, five months after the end of the war, my brother Gerd was born, and on Ash Wednesday, February 11, 1948, I joined him. The Schröder family was now complete.

And the house became full! Back then, four generations of our family lived under one roof: my great-grandparents, my grandmother and her sister, my parents and finally my brother and me. There were also occasional housemates. Due to the massive destruction of living space during the war, the house owners were obliged to take in additional tenants. So; there were at least nine of us in the house. Soon afterwards, in 1949, my great-grandfather, the old pastor Friedrich, left us at the age of 90. His wife Sophie followed him five years later, in 1954.

By all accounts, Friedrich probably saved my life, the house and perhaps the whole family. The story goes that he was in the attic one day when an incendiary bomb - a popular weapon of the British military at the time - smashed through the roof and landed in the attic. The old man bravely grabbed the bomb before it could ignite and threw it back into the garden through the hole in the roof. The pictures of countless burnt-down houses in major German cities show what could have happened if the wooden floor of the attic had caught fire. Friedrich became my hero. On the whole, I survived the turmoil of war relatively unscathed, apart from a few insignificant cracks in the brickwork. Most of the houses in the immediate vicinity fared in the same way. In other parts of the city, however, there was severe destruction.

On the whole, the relationship between the two siblings Luise and Mathilde was very harmonious, even if it was not always easy. This may have been due to the division of tasks and the perceived authority of the older sister, teacher and landlady. Luise lived in what is now the dining room on the ground floor as her study and bedroom, while Mathilde occupied the beautiful corner room on the first floor. Both ladies had a piano in their rooms, which they loved to play. Although their musical preferences were by no means the same, they occasionally tried a really daring experiment, playing four-handed. This often went wrong, but the siblings showed amazing perseverance in trying again and again.

Living in Times of Scarcity

The garden in her house was an essential part of Luise's new life. Neatly laid out paths strewn with gravel ran through it like a park. Her pride and joy, however, were her rose beds along the paths. Here the roses were cultivated, pruned and cared for with scientific meticulousness. When they bloomed, they were admired by the whole family. In addition, the garden was always an important source of food for the family during the Second World War and in the barren years that followed. There was a lot of fruit, several apple trees, a peach tree, a mirabelle plum tree, a cherry tree and a plum tree. There were also bushes of black and red currants, gooseberries, raspberries and a strawberry patch. In the middle of the garden were the vegetable patches, in wooden crates and some with glass covers. Lettuce, peas, beans, carrots, cucumbers and herbs grew here. However, the garden was dominated by the chicken enclosure, which took up a large corner of the garden. It consisted of a small house with a ladder for the chickens. There were a few square meters of run around the house. The garden and the chicken coop are among my earliest childhood memories. I liked the chickens and believed that they felt at home there, which was perhaps true. I was also a specialist at stealing eggs from the protected henhouse. So, I could always proudly present "my" yield to Grandma Mathilde. Dad had also built a swing, and a hammock could be set up between the fruit trees, inviting us to rest and dream. Later, the fruit trees were a tempting place to climb, to harvest the fruit or simply to eat it on the spot in the tree.

Overall, the food situation for the large family in the post-war years was anything but good. In photos of my parents from that time, I can see how frighteningly emaciated they both were. Yet they were actually in a privileged situation, at least compared to other families in the city. The large garden provided fruit and vegetables, the chicken coop eggs and occasionally meat. The greatest privilege, however, was my parents' scientific talent, which always paid off in real potatoes, a necessary part of our diet. Some of the fruit, especially gooseberries and currants, was processed into delicious fruit wine. For further processing, Dad built a distillery from laboratory equipment, which produced a tasty schnapps from the wine. This was very popular with the local farmers. Dad would often swap his schnapps for a good portion of potatoes, which he would then bring home in his handcart. The schnapps production gave off its aroma both inside and outside the house and was certainly not entirely legal. But who asked for it in those days?

Childlike Experiences

I was quite fat in my early years, which is amazing when you consider how scarce food was back then. But I was probably, as I was told, very fixated on my own diet, especially the supply of meat. It was rare back then and usually a chicken from our own chicken farm was sacrificed for it. Grandmother Mathilde was responsible for that. She disappeared into the chicken enclosure with a sack in her hand and stuffed the chosen chicken backwards into the sack so that only the head was sticking out. Then, with calm composure, she reached for a kitchen cleaver and severed the head from the chicken with one blow. I still remember the poor animal flapping for what felt like minutes (it was probably only seconds) before the sack was quiet. Then the feathers were plucked out and the remaining bristles burned over the gas stove. The smell of the burnt bristles was unpleasant, but at the same time aroused the anticipation of a delicious meat dish.

Most of the time, however, we only had potatoes and vegetables or whatever else the sparse food market had to offer, often in the form of soup. I still had difficulties with the word meat ("Fleisch") back then, it sounded more like "Beisch". But I did miss it. My searching glance across the laid table and the anxious question "Beisch, where are you?" were part of the family's treasure trove of oft-quoted anecdotes for years. I also liked to share my observations and analysis of the surroundings with the family during this time. One such basic insight, which was also often quoted, related to the interplay between the time of day and lighting conditions: "It's dark in the evening and light in the morning".

It was probably not only because of my sparse meat consumption that I was rather slender from school age onwards. My thin arms and legs earned me the nickname "Krake" (octopus) from my classmates. Even as an adult, my weight remained under 60 kg for a long time. This changed fundamentally when I turned 40 and started living with my wife Cecilia, but more on that later.

He certainly didn't like the nickname Krake at first! Later, however, he adopted the name and made it his personal trademark. His preference for planning and organizing trips himself, with all the necessary research, became the kraketravel brand. Under this brand, he not only organized trips for himself and his professional activities, but also for his family and friends. The pictures and rather professionally designed videos of these trips bore the brand name krakemedia. In this way, he even managed to turn a mocking name into something positive.

I belong to a complex of three houses and am the southern end-terrace house. When I was built, there was no sewage system in this street. Instead, the wastewater was channel led into a pit in the garden about eight meters deep, the so-called soakaway. From there, the solids that didn't seep away were collected from time to time by a tanker from the FäKa company. The three soakaways for the three houses were all located in our garden to make removal easier. In the 1950s, our street was finally canalized and the deep pits in the garden became superfluous.

I don't remember what fascinated me so much about this dirty work as a child, but the FäKa campaign always had my undivided attention. Laying the metal pipes and thick hoses for the bends up to the pits and then the actual extraction process - the technical interest obviously outweighed the penetrating stench. Fortunately, the future engineer's interest soon shifted to other technical developments. When the pits became superfluous thanks to the sewer system, we were able to fill them with all kinds of useless or superfluous things. There was no regulated bulky waste collection at that time. So, we took the opportunity to thoroughly clear out the house, especially the cellar and attic, and put everything we no longer needed into the pits. In fact, these were completely sealed in the following years. But even today, the pits still sink a little from time to time and are then filled with topsoil to avoid tripping hazards in the garden.

A New Home in Cologne

Finally, it was time for the young Schröder family to leave the house. Dad had already found work in a beverage company in Cologne in December 1945. After a period of commuting between Düsseldorf and Cologne, he was able to rent an apartment for the family in Cologne. So, the family moved from Düsseldorf to Cologne, Dad's old home city. His tasks in the beverage company were recipe development and quality control of the drinks. He was to hold this position his entire professional life, with growing responsibility and increasing management functions.

So, I spent my school years in Cologne until I graduated from high school. However, I always kept in touch with my parents' house in Düsseldorf. Visits to Grandma Mathilde and Aunt Luise were still a regular part of the program and were very popular. Like my brother Gerd, I had my own room in the house. These two rooms, connected by a passageway, are the only rooms in the otherwise empty and unfinished attic on the second floor. Above them, under the peak of the roof, there is another wooden loft that can only be reached via a ladder and can only be accessed by small people. Both rooms had no heating at that time, so it could get bitterly cold in winter. I still remember the ice flowers that adorned the small windows. I also remember the hot water bottle in the bed, which alternately warmed my back and my feet after getting into bed. Instead of looking into the fog when we exhaled, we quickly learned to channel the warm air under the comforter towards our stomachs. As cold as it was in winter, the nights directly under the roof could get hot in summer. But none of this detracted from the joy of our frequent visits to our house in Düsseldorf. It was always a wonderful experience.

As the Schröder family didn't have a car at the time, we traveled between cities by train. When I was about ten years old, I was allowed to travel to Düsseldorf by train on my own for the first time. The trains had steam engines and exuded an atmosphere that fascinated me. After the electrification of the line, the new electric locomotives made it even more exciting for me. Before and after the journey, I always wanted to stay at the station for a while to watch the arriving and departing trains. The absolute highlight was the diesel-powered TEE (Trans Europe Express), a fast and comfortable train that was of course far too expensive for me to ride myself. I became a member of the Pfiff Club of railroad enthusiasts and was given a membership card with the number 700. No train driver was safe from me, and eventually I really found one who let me ride on his electric locomotive on the route from Düsseldorf to Cologne - with a valid ticket, of course.

For me, the house, the "Cologne period" was a quiet time without any major changes. Mathilde took care of the household and Luise looked after the garden. After dinner, usually with sandwiches, a pot of tea with a little sugar was put on for the evening together. There was no television at first; the old ladies used to go to bed early so that they could perhaps read something before going to sleep. It wasn't until later that the huge box of a new tube TV was set up in my living room. Otherwise, the ladies were happy about the regular visits from Cologne, where there was always lots to talk about.

School Days in Cologne

My school days began after Easter 1954 at the Cologne-Bayental elementary school. To get to school I had to cross a busy main road, which was no problem after appropriate instruction and with the help of school crossing guards. My first teacher, Mrs. Oster, was a friendly and empathetic woman. Her husband, also a teacher at this school, had already taught Gerd. In 1956, the family moved to a larger apartment in Cologne-Dellbrück. For me, this meant a change of school, which caused me a few sleepless nights, but then went quite smoothly. In my new class, I particularly liked a girl with blonde pigtails, Hannelore. She sat on the bench in front of me and we both competed for the status of best in class.

However, this status came to an abrupt end when I moved to the grammar school in Cologne-Deutz in 1958. The standards there were much higher than at elementary school, so I tended to perform in the lower middle of the class. Only boys were taught at the grammar school, which even became somewhat famous during the carnival season as the "Düxer Ströpp". One teacher in particular was very involved in the carnival, and on his initiative, the school even held its own carnival sessions. A music teacher organized his own school band to provide the appropriate atmosphere. Incidentally, the nearest girls' high school was just around the corner.

There were hardly any peers in the immediate vicinity of our apartment. But a few streets away, on a hill between a forest and a small heath, there was an attractive new housing estate. I met Dirk there and we soon became best friends. Later, Christoph and Edwin from other new builds joined us. We met up almost every afternoon and passed the time in the grounds, on our bikes or with a shared but rather unsuccessful crush on a girl from the neighborhood, Roswitha. Only Dirk, the proud owner of a small but cozy garden shed, seemed to be hiding something from us...

Musically, the French singer Françoise Hardy made a big impression on me back then. Her simple, very romantic and always somewhat melancholy songs were mostly about longing and the search for love, which was pretty much exactly how I felt at the time. I was a loyal Françoise fan, had autograph cards and posters, and the beautiful and not much older singer often appeared in my dreams. I had no idea at the time: The search for love and romance would occupy an important place in my life for a long time to come. But the accompanying music changed: soon after Françoise Hardy, it was the Rolling Stones who articulated my feelings.

Christoph and I were real cycling fanatics and often rode the 8 km or so to Deutz grammar school together. In bad weather, we also took the streetcar or Christoph's father put us in his Opel. Soon we were together every day. Wild maneuvers on the bike were also part of our free time. For us, purposeful skidding didn't mean danger, but pleasure. I overturned my bike twice without any serious injuries - and without a helmet, which was not yet mandatory at the time. Mother had long since got used to cooking also for Christoph after the school run. We made a clever strategy out of this and often went for another lunch at Christoph's mother's house afterwards. After a few years, Christoph switched from a grammar school for modern languages in Deutz to a science grammar school because he saw his strengths there. Dirk took a different path and gradually lost contact. He died a few years later in a car accident.

Over the years, Christoph's and my interests shifted from the grounds and bicycles to more activities in the house. Hi-fi quality music systems played a major role in this. And, of course, parties with various partners, mostly from the dance school. From today's perspective, these "parties" seem downright frighteningly well-behaved. The approach to the coveted girls was very tentative on both sides, more like trial and error with a lot of mistakes. One reason for this was certainly that sex education - unthinkable for my parents - was practically non-existent in the mostly very prudish homes. Not so with Christoph's mother: she was aware of my cramped living conditions at home and, in a confidential conversation, offered me the opportunity to use her guest room with a friend if necessary. Even though I was rather embarrassed by this offer at the time and never took her up on it, I still admire her today for her empathy and willingness to help. An unusual and courageous gesture of friendship in those uptight times, which might even have made her liable to prosecution.

Dad had developed a passion for theme parties with his old friends, in which the whole family actively participated. For example, there was a Western saloon where Christoph and I liked to take part in the whisky tasting in the appropriate setting and get-up. The subsequent photo of Christoph with a glowing head is part of family history. The first moon landing, which Christoph and I watched all night while lying on a couple of pillows in front of the TV, is also unforgettable - Christoph's parents already had a color TV.

When my parents weren't at home, we sometimes had a secret evening get-together in front of the otherwise rather restrictive TV. This opportunity presented itself every two weeks on Tuesday evenings, as the parents then regularly attended a dance circle. The occasional highlight was a homemade punch. A cheap wine from the kiosk, a few spoons of sugar and a jar of preserved fruit and the delicious, because forbidden, product was ready. By today's standards, it was more of a culinary nightmare.

None of us were high-flyers at school. Some subjects, such as history, were simply not my thing. As early as the third grade (quarta), I got a slap in the face from my history teacher with the comment that I would probably never pass the Abitur. Motivation looks different. Somehow, however, I managed to get through my time at school without any "honor rounds", even if it was a bit tight at times. I managed to pass my Abitur, but only with a mediocre average grade. Christoph had successfully solved his problems with foreign languages by switching to the science grammar school. This enabled him to meet the requirements for studying medicine with a respectable A-level average. Gerd also struggled at first. However, a tactical change of school to another grammar school in Düsseldorf saved the day. Instead, he moved and lived in our Düsseldorf house again for a year. As an experienced teacher, Aunt Luise probably kept a watchful eye on his progress there. Once the situation had stabilized, he moved back to the grammar school in Cologne-Deutz. However, he also increasingly struggled with foreign languages. He was constantly at war with his French teacher in particular. When no solution emerged during the war, he left the Deutz grammar school with a technical college entrance qualification to begin his engineering training after an internship.

A Wonderful Teenage Playground

Even during his time at grammar school, there were always reasons to visit our house in Düsseldorf. Grandmother Mathilde often rewarded particularly good grades in class tests or school reports with a small donation. And the opportunities and freedom in the house were simply much greater than in the room in our apartment that I shared with Gerd. Grandma Mathilde and Aunt Luise were very generous and tolerant during these visits.

Christoph also came to Düsseldorf occasionally and was always a welcome guest, even with the old ladies. Our favorite places were the cellar and especially the attic, where Gerd and I also had our rooms. We passed the time listening to music and making music ourselves with all kinds of instruments and drums. Bizarre photos based on the pop art of the time were also on the agenda. We painted the walls of the attic rooms with sometimes funny, sometimes dark sayings and drawings of vintage cars, flowers and stylized bombs from the hippie and subsequent underground era - an exuberant and pubescent confrontation with the zeitgeist.

Only the noise had to be kept within limits in the attic, as the thin wooden floor offered no effective sound insulation from the grandmother's bedroom below. Anything loud was better off in the cellar. There was another special feature: the shelves still contained the remains of the old gooseberry wine that Dad had made into fruit brandy in the post-war period and then exchanged for potatoes from the farmer. This brew suited our preference for sweet drinks at the time. We didn't drink much, but it always had a quick effect. Our musical performances then lost some of their harmony but gained in volume. We were left to our own devices. In the old house we were allowed to "let off steam", to be harmlessly playful and somehow happy teenagers. At home, on the other hand, things were much stricter in both families.

His room ~ oh my God! The wallpaper should have been replaced long ago. But they remained, because of the "works of art", an early form of private graffiti. The drawings were less sensational, more like caricatures, the lyrics were often taken from songs by Bob Dylan or the Rolling Stones, and in between there were his own productions in the form of poems. An advertising poster with nuns in an Afri-Cola frenzy, which was as popular as it was controversial at the time, fitted perfectly into the picture. Nostalgic feelings about this carefree time ensured that the overall work of art remained intact for many years, until finally the urgently needed insulation required the demolition of the now slightly rotten wallpaper. I had nothing against it!

The Rocky Road to Becoming an Engineer

In October 1966, it was finally done - the Abitur! The long and not always pleasant school days were over. But there was no thought of vacations and relaxation.

A trip abroad after leaving school, perhaps combined with a social year, was not so common at the time and was not within our financial means. There was no rest for me after graduating from high school. The new semester at Aachen Technical University began just a few days after graduating. My Dad had more or less made the decision for me to study engineering there.

I had thought more about medicine, but my A-level average wasn't good enough for that. The few days until the start of the semester were short enough to find an apartment in a student residence and enrol at the university. In many ways, it was like jumping in at the deep end. On the one hand, I was happy to be able to leave my parents' home and parental paternalism at the age of just 18. On the other hand, I wasn't at all used to standing on my own two feet. This brought with it insecurities and it took me a while to gain my own experience.

In addition, my financial resources were very limited. My Dad gave me about half the BAföG-rate per month that was valid at the time, which students whose parents were unable to finance their studies received from the state. That was just enough to live in a student hall of residence and eat in the canteen. However, the hall of residence was only available as a temporary solution for first-year students. When I had to move out after two semesters, the budget was nowhere near enough for a normal student room. I finally found a small room in a shack in the backyard with a bed, an armchair and a coal stove. There was a sink, but no bathroom, and the only toilet for several tenants was in the outbuilding. For larger transactions, I preferred to go to the nearby lecture hall building for good reason. In hindsight, it was probably a good thing that my parents never saw this dwelling.

After all, the degree itself was awesome! With my education from a modern language grammar school, I initially understood almost nothing in the mathematics lecture. It was the same in "Theoretical Electrical Engineering". The professors wrote endless formulas on the blackboard, which I struggled to write down without understanding anything. Unfortunately, at first, I couldn't find a suitable working group to work through the difficult material together with fellow students. In general, social contacts were difficult in this environment, not least because of my miserable accommodation and the chronic shortage of money. This left only the official university tutorials to cope with the material. Despite this, I made a few friends, but the rare evenings at the Greek restaurant were only enough for a beer and a plate of rice with sauce. As expected, I failed the exams in the two difficult subjects, but luckily, I was able to revise the material. That was enough to just about pass the re-exams, so I could continue my studies without losing any time.

But even in this very modest living environment, it was possible to have a bit of fun. As a technology student, I knew that normal boiled sausages represent a resistor from an electrical point of view. So, if you pass electricity through such a sausage, it gets hot. So, we connected our sausages to the socket via two carbon electrodes and, with a few bottles of beer and a tube of mustard, watched our unusual cooking success with amusement. Even the slight chlorine taste caused by the electrical decomposition didn't put us off. We also shared our discovery and enjoyment with a few passers-by. Some friends had traveled all the way from Cologne.

According to my parents, the regular commute between Aachen and Cologne was supposed to be by train. However, they hadn't considered that the meagre monthly budget they gave me was barely enough for food and accommodation. It certainly didn't include travel costs. So, I was occasionally lucky enough to get a lift in a car from fellow students, but mostly I hitchhiked. That usually went well, and it was quite entertaining to talk to strangers for an hour or so once a week. Only once did a gay man drop me off on the hard shoulder of the highway because I didn't want to respond to his advances. But somehow, even in this situation, I found a driver who came to my rescue and picked me up on the hard shoulder. Luckily it wasn't a policeman.

From the fifth semester onwards, the situation became a little more relaxed. Now I also had time to supplement my tight budget with small part-time jobs. I tutored high school students in mathematics and physics. I also found cheap accommodation by one of my tutoring students in his parents' house. After a while, I was even able to get my driving license and buy my first car. It was a second-hand and rather old Citroën 2CV, the popular student car that you could repair a lot yourself. The car also made it easier for me to find a better apartment, as I was now able to consider cheaper offers a little further away. I decided on a large room in an old moated castle in Belgium near the border, the Château de Ruyff in Henri Chapelle. The castle belonged to the Catholic Church and was administered by a priest. He lived in the left wing of the building, while he rented out the right "sinful" wing to students at a reasonable price. The little-used main road from Aachen to the small town of Henri Chapelle led past a secluded quarry pond, which was perfect for an after-work swim in the summer. At first, I stopped at the border, later I learned that you didn't even have to change down, it was always free flowing.

Having my own car also made the weekly commute home much easier. My parents' reactions varied. Dad, who hadn't bought his first car until he was about 40, thought it was inappropriate to own a car as a student. Mother, on the other hand, was delighted because I enjoyed driving her to the shops at the weekend. She thanked me with occasional fill-ups, which weren't that expensive back then - the benefit was mutual.

A Brief Interlude in the Past

After many years in apartments in Cologne, most recently in Cologne-Dellbrück, Dad finally wanted to fulfill his dream of owning his own house in 1968. He opted for an unusual new-build project, a round house on three steel legs that was more reminiscent of a spaceship. The planned location in Sinnersdorf, a rather remote community in the rural outskirts of Cologne, was not exactly met with enthusiasm by the younger generation, i.e. my brother Gerd and me. But then the construction of the futuristic group of houses took much longer than originally planned, so that Dad ran out of time with his planning. The apartment in Cologne-Dellbrück had already been given notice, the moving date was approaching, and the completion of the new building was still out of the question. There were probably technical problems with the unconventional construction, perhaps also with the financing of the project. Dad somehow managed to get out of the contract. He soon found a new building project, this time a classic end-terrace house in Brühl-Vochem.

However, this didn't solve the problem of us having to move out of our apartment, which we had already given notice on. An offer from Aunt Luise came at just the right time to put us up in her house again for the transitional period until the new house was ready. I was already living in Aachen at the time, but I came home almost every weekend, not least because I really appreciated my mother's laundry service. So, we vacated our apartment in Cologne-Dellbrück and moved back to Düsseldorf with all our belongings. The house was filling up again.

And there they were again! No longer the young family with two small children, but now an established married couple with two sons who were already quite independent students. Everyday life in the house was now very different from before. A constant coming and going was the norm, especially at weekends. Things were quieter during the week, when the two budding engineers studied at their universities in Cologne and Aachen and Dad made his daily commute to work in Cologne. But it wasn't to last that long, as the new building in Brühl was making good progress.

A Failed Adventure

From about the age of 14, I had a few international penfriendships, particularly with two French girls and an English girl. At the time, pen pals were like the WhatsApp of my generation at that age. Among other things, the letters contained more or less intense expressions of friendship, which were reinforced by an international code of symbols, comparable to today's emoticons. Most of them were virtual kisses and a vague indication of where to place them.

Nicole lived near Paris and wanted to make a short detour to Düsseldorf to visit me on her way to relatives in Germany. Although the house was quite full at the time we were passing through, I got permission to put Nicole up in a small guest room for two nights one weekend. She arrived in Düsseldorf shortly after me and we spent a fun afternoon with the family. In view of the full house, I kissed her goodnight at her door without any ulterior motives. But after years of good virtual preparation, Nicole had more of an internship in mind. She pulled me into her room without further ado and closed the door forcefully - a brief moment that cast my previous expectations of the rest of the evening in a completely new light. But we had not reckoned with my mother; our happiness lasted a minute at most. My mother had been watching the scene from the stairs and started knocking loudly on the door. When I didn't open it immediately, she threw a little tantrum. The mood was gone, the situation was hopeless and there was no hope of a French adventure. Such an adventure probably didn't fit into my mother's world view either - or was it perhaps a little jealousy?

In any case, there was no second attempt, and the day after next a somewhat frustrated French girl left the house. The pen pal relationship with Nicole ended a little later.

I would have loved to have given them both this little experience within my walls! The mutual discovery, the curious kisses and touches, it probably wouldn't have been much more in the given situation. And all this in the necessary silence, with the tingling attraction of the secret and the constant danger of the family noticing something. An adventure and a little piece of youthful happiness.

Dad's New House

In 1970, the time had finally come: the new house in Brühl-Vochem was finished and ready to move into. Or rather: almost finished. The front garden had not yet been laid out, and the only way to the front door was a narrow, sloping footbridge over an impressive landscape of clay and mud - a challenge for the entire moving team, including us. But we proudly dragged our things inside and began to put them away. With every unpacked box, the house became more familiar and homely. Dad made a point of planting two birch trees in the garden so that they blocked the view of our terrace from a neighboring apartment building. It still took a lot of joint family work in the house and garden before the permanent building site was finished and the house shone in its new beauty.

Dad had really done it; the family's new home was their own house! The new owners settled in proudly and happily. But their unadulterated happiness did not last long. The very next year was to be a very difficult one for the family.

Peace and quiet returned to my own four walls after the family's move, and the two old ladies were able to recover a little after the turbulent months of our family interlude. There were no changes for me either during this time due to renovations or conversions. Life went on in a calm, orderly fashion in my now somewhat worn-out building and furnishings.

Flower Power Love

During my studies in Aachen, I regularly commuted home almost every weekend, first to Cologne-Dellbrück, then to Düsseldorf during the transition period and later to Brühl-Vochem. I met Brigitte in Cologne and became friends with her. We were indeed a funny long-haired couple, my hair straight with the first clear highlights on the infamous receding hairline, hers long and rather wild. Although we both came from very conservative homes, we shared an eye for the burgeoning hippie culture of the time. With the music of Bob Dylan, Joan Baez and the Rolling Stones, we at least enjoyed the rather harmless trappings of the flower power movement: Colorful clothes in "shock colors", bell bottoms and the obligatory flokati coat. Although it kept us nice and warm, it was best not to wear it in the rain because it would give off an intense smell of sheep. Brigitte and I had a beautiful, light, spring-like and very romantic love affair, but - as it turned out later - it was also not very resilient and hardly suitable for everyday life. But we didn't really think about that at the time.

The Fateful Year 1971

With my new home in Brühl-Vochem, I was back in the Cologne area more often. This and the prospect of soon graduating from university intensified my romantic relationship with Brigitte, so that the question of marriage soon arose. Without hesitation, we both said yes to each other and surprised Brigitte's mother with the news while baking a crumble cake. While her head was still processing the news, her hand continued to sprinkle, giving the cake more crumble than ever before. The engagement party took place on September 11, 1971, in glorious weather on the terrace of the new Schröder house in Brühl-Vochem. Brigitte wore a long dress she had sewn herself and my tie was made from the same fabric. It was a happy family celebration.

But only a few weeks later came the darkest day of my life. On the urgent advice of Christoph's father, a medical officer in Cologne, my mother was admitted to Bonn University Hospital the next day due to chronic shortness of breath. She died there completely unexpectedly the following night, on November 24, 1971. The news from the clinic hit us sons and Dad like a bolt from the blue. We rushed to the hospital in Bonn from different directions. I was the first to arrive, stayed at my mother's deathbed for maybe five minutes, then I couldn't stand it there any longer. I said goodbye to my mother forever and waited in the corridor for the others. The sight of my dead mother is etched in my memory, the image is still as fresh today as it was then. Dad and

Gerd arrived shortly afterwards and also said goodbye. Dad was crying. I drove us home in Dad´s car, in silence, lost in thought. At home, three men were sitting in the living room, struggling with grief and tears and had no idea what to do next. They all became painfully aware that mother had run the household almost single-handedly and had always been the center of the family. The gap that suddenly opened up was huge. We had a lot to deal with, from the preparations for the funeral to the reorganization of the household. For example, nobody knew exactly how the washing machine worked, least of all Dad. Gerd was the first to get to grips with it.

And we had one worry: How were we going to tell Grandma Mathilde and Aunt Luise? We needed a night to get our heads together. The next morning, we were in the car on our difficult journey to Düsseldorf. It fell to me to go in and tell her. Grandma Mathilde was shocked but remained very calm. After a few minutes, she went to the door and called the others in. Together we remembered our mother, her only daughter, and stayed until the evening. Grandmother Mathilde found comfort with her sister Luise.

The funeral at the beautiful forest cemetery in Vochem, just a few hundred meters from our new house, was the terrible climax of this family drama. We were stunned to see the coffin being lowered into the grave. The traditional coffee table that followed was torture. I would have preferred to remain alone with my grief.

1971 was a fateful year for the family. Mother's death hit us all hard. We were able to overcome the despair, but the grief remained. And the impending marriage to Brigitte was not under a good star either, it didn't last long. But there was also good news: Gerd started working as an engineer at Siemens that year, the beginning of an extremely successful career. He remained loyal to the company until his retirement.

A Beginning Without Magic

Life went on. In February 1972, Gerd and Juliane got engaged, and on May 23, 1972, Brigitte and I got married. The wedding in the small chapel of Schnellenberg Castle in Attendorn suited our playful, romantic relationship well. The subsequent lunch in the castle's Knights' Hall was another lovely family celebration, even though the grief for Mother was always present.

On January 20, 1973, there was another wedding: Dad and Gretel, a former neighbor from our time in Cologne-Dellbrück. The wedding came as something of a surprise for us, but in the end, we were all glad that Dad no longer had to live alone. Gerd and Juliane finally tied the knot on February 23, 1973.

On June 20, 1972, I received my diploma in engineering. I had already applied for July 1, 1972, as a research assistant at the University of Essen. But then Brigitte and

I made a fatal decision. Of course, the obvious thing to do was to accept Aunt Luise's invitation and move into the house in Düsseldorf, just a twenty-minute drive from my new workplace. But it wasn't a wise idea. The household in my former parental home ran according to the long-established rules of the two old ladies. Grandma Mathilde and Aunt Luise had their cherished habits. Changes and innovations were hardly welcome here. And then a young woman came into the house who had her own and often very different ideas about the house and household. We used my later office on the first floor as the living room and the small guest room as the dining room. Our bedroom and another small room were in the attic. We shared the kitchen and bathroom with the two old ladies. Our rooms soon shone in new colors; colorful, large-patterned and eye-catching wallpaper was all the rage at the time. Our dining room had a rustic solid wood table decorated at the front by a frame made of railroad sleepers. The wall behind it was a dark turquoise color. In the kitchen, an old, yellowed cupboard was unceremoniously painted dark green.

However, the fresh colors could not hide the fact that there were problems in the house, even though there was a good will to live together harmoniously on both sides. For example, it proved difficult to use the kitchen together without disturbing Grandma Mathilde's well-established kitchen rituals. The old ladies' need for peace and quiet was also not always easy to respect when living closely with the young couple and their friends. The dining room adjoined Mathilde's bedroom, and when friends came to eat, it was not allowed to be noisy.

Children were out of the question in this complicated situation anyway. Brigitte wasn't happy in this house, even if she didn't let on at first. And in hindsight, I must reproach myself for greatly underestimating this problem. Moving into our own apartment would have been the only right solution.

I was delighted that the young couple had chosen me as their new home. And the renovation and freshening up of their rooms did me good. So, I was all the sadder when I realized that, despite all the good will on both sides to live together harmoniously, the situation was ultimately unsatisfactory for all four residents. And if people don't feel comfortable within my walls, then it's also unpleasant for me as a house. I would certainly have been sad if the couple had decided to move to another apartment. But it was even sadder for me to watch this young marriage slowly fall apart.

There were other problems too. The romance faded and everyday life caught up with us. My work took up a lot of my time. Brigitte, on the other hand, only found a half-time job as a social worker. She taught ikebana on the side. Our interests became more sober and grew apart. The flower power era was over. Everyday married life was still harmonious, but slowly became routine. Leisure activities became more valuable due to the lack of time, including meetings with friends. I bought an old two-seater VW buggy, which we had a lot of fun with and also went on nice trips. But it was Grandma Mathilde who had the most fun with this open beach buggy. She enjoyed it when we drove slowly through the town in the open car and people turned around and waved at the old lady in the buggy. Aunt Luise was a stranger to such pleasures. When she sat in the car with me, she insisted on closing the roof.

But the funny car also had its pitfalls. I often had to get under the car with a screwdriver to start it and bridge a contact because the starter cable was faulty. The beach car also had no heating and was quite leaky. I drilled a hole in the floor so that the water could run off when it rained. After the first winter, I didn't feel like driving in glacier gear any more. The buggy was sold.

What a symbol! The fun car is sold and at the same time the young couple's hippie days are obviously coming to an end. But this lightness had been their trademark and what they had in common. And another big test is still to come...

A Silent Heroine Leaves

Finally, Aunt Luise became ill and needed more and more help and care, for example at night on the toilet. A bell was installed that could be switched either to grandmother or to us. It was to Brigitte's credit that she took an active part in caring for the elderly aunt despite our difficulties. Grandmother, aunt and I were very grateful to her for this and showed it. It was often exhausting, but we all took it for granted that the old lady could stay in her own home until the end. Aunt Luise died peacefully in her bed at night in 1973.

It was not an easy life, which at least came to a dignified end here. Luise never had it easy, and many things in her life went against her. In her childhood and youth, she was strictly ruled, and her own wishes and ideas were hardly considered. Following her career aspirations, she would probably have become a good nurse or found fulfillment in an artistic profession. But she was determined to become a teacher, even though she disliked school life. She followed the instructions and requirements with great discipline, but she was ultimately unable to cope with the many stresses and strains. The constant excessive demands made her depressed and, as a result, physically ill. Only cures lasting several months with plenty of time for her artistic inclinations were able to restore her spirits. This was aggravated by the turmoil of the First World War and the equally difficult post-war period with miserable living and housing conditions. Only by chance (or providence?) was her artist friend able to prevent the fatal conclusion of her collapse. But they were also denied the fulfillment of their love. That's where I came into play, my construction gave her a big task and her life a perspective again. Living with her family within my walls fulfilled and enriched her. So, everything could have turned out well. But fate intervened in her life again: The Second World War rewrote her story and presented her and her family with the toughest of challenges. She was only allowed to spend the last twenty years of her life in modest prosperity in a harmonious family circle in her own, self-built house. Luise was a silent heroine, a model of human kindness and self-discipline. After her peaceful death, she was laid to rest in the nearby Protestant cemetery. She will never be forgotten within my walls.

The death of her sister did not come as a surprise to Grandmother Mathilde. However, after decades of living with her sister, it was a drastic change in her life. Many cherished habits and rituals were gone. Above all, she now missed the constant exchange of thoughts and feelings with her sister. Of course, it was now our job to compensate for this deficit, at least in part. Grandma Mathilde now was even more integrated into our everyday lives.

Finally Studying Medicine

In 1976, I made a difficult but very important decision for my future career: I began to study medicine in Düsseldorf. It wasn't easy to get there as I couldn't score well with my A-levels. The only option was a small second-degree quota. This required recommendations from two university lecturers. My boss in Essen, Professor Klosterkötter, expressly encouraged me to take this step. I then received a second recommendation from Professor Effert in Cologne. But even that didn't clear the way to university, because the University of Düsseldorf refused additional places. In the end, however, it had to bow to a temporary injunction from the Gelsenkirchen Administrative Court. Once again, the requirements were only secured a few days before I started my studies, which took place in the winter semester of 1976/77.

He would have preferred to start studying medicine straight after his A-levels, but this failed due to his mediocre A-levels, which did not meet the numerus-clausus criteria for medicine. However, studying engineering as a substitute was also okay for him. The decisive turning point that led to his decision to study medicine as a second degree was the death of his mother. It subsequently turned out that she had ended up in this dangerous situation due to years of incorrect treatment by her GP, which then led to her death. The doctor had treated her increasing breathlessness as asthma and failed to recognize that the real cause was a fatal heart condition. This could and should have been treated very differently. It became clear that his mother should not have died so early. The family doctor was informed by the clinic about the course of the disease but was not prepared to discuss it. This behavior shocked the family. His mother could not be brought back to life, but it was here that his decision to study medicine in order to do better later on matured.

As promising as the decision to study medicine was for my future career, it proved fatal for my already strained marriage. There were additional problems of a financial and time-related nature. Of course, I had to give up my job at the University of Essen and my salary was lost. To compensate, Professor Klosterkötter had arranged two jobs for me in Düsseldorf, as managing director of the

German Working Group for Noise Abatement (DAL) and as editor of the "Zeitschrift für Lärmbekämpfung". I was able to do both jobs flexibly and therefore alongside my studies. But my overall income was now significantly lower than before. However, I was able to compensate for this deficit to some extent by working as a substitute physics teacher at a grammar school. The second problem was that the new degree course and these three part-time jobs put a lot of pressure on my time. There were only a few hours a week for our life together and it didn't get any better. We were taking big steps in different directions.

A house is often the scene for dramatic decisions and conflict situations. Sometimes decisions have to be made in life that are of great importance for the future. You stand at a crossroads and see various options for continuing on your path. In most cases, the alternatives have different advantages and disadvantages that have to be weighed up against each other. In this case, certain professional advantages were set against the further strain on an already strained marriage. In essence, the decision to study had already been made much earlier, there was just a lack of opportunity. In retrospect, the question arises: what would have happened if the decision had been different? In this case in particular, where the breakdown of the marriage followed almost immediately after the decision to study, this question comes to mind. Could the marriage have been saved? And if so, at what cost?

The End of Flower Power

In 1977, the inevitable happened. After long, sad discussions, but without a war of the roses, we looked for a new apartment for Brigitte. She left the house. There wasn't much to divide up in this student-led marriage. But, among other things, she really wanted to take our wonderful 240x200 mattress with her. Transporting this unwieldy item to her apartment was a logistical challenge, but with a lot of cord and tape, we managed to solve the problem ourselves in the end.

Obviously, we both needed some time out after this turmoil. Inspired by an old movie about the dream road Panamericana, I planned a trip to Peru, a country that was completely unknown to me until then. The cheap flight was due to take off from Zurich on July 18, 1978. Brigitte had actually planned a stay in Switzerland for the same date. So, we went to Zurich together by car. There we went our separate ways. My flight arrived in Lima at midnight, where I initially stood at the airport without speaking a word of Spanish. With some effort, I still managed to find accommodation and plan the next few days. This stay in Peru with all its experiences and new friendships helped me out of my first divorce slump, gave me new inspiration and ideas and was very formative for me and my future life. I will write more about this later. Peru is still a very special country for me today.

In the meantime, the divorce proceedings were underway at home. As there was no longer any dispute between us in this matter, we decided to hire a joint lawyer for the proceedings - also for cost reasons, of course. We went to the court hearing hand in hand and the lawyer sat between us at the hearing. As peaceful and amicable as we were at the hearing, the final verdict hit us both hard: our marriage was divorced in the name of the people on the grounds of breakdown! The romantic and playful hippie era was finally over. Although we hadn't wished it any other way, we left the court feeling rather dejected. We spent the next hour in a nearby café trying to come to terms with the impact of the verdict; it wasn't easy. Very thoughtful days and weeks followed for both of us. The divorce decree became final on March 30, 1979.

Living Alone with Grandma

It didn't make things any easier at home either: I was now alone in the house with Grandma Mathilde. Things went well at first, but the old lady got weaker and weaker. She ate and drank more and more irregularly, so I also had to take care of her meals, which I even managed to do to some extent.

But small successes sometimes make you overconfident. The new "chef" in my kitchen had to learn this too. Christmas was just around the corner, and it had always been a family tradition to celebrate Christmas Day with a big lunch together in the living room of my old home. But the previous organizers of this feast, Mathilde and Brigitte, could no longer or no longer wanted to. "No problem", said the new "chef" and invited the whole family to a goose dinner on Christmas Day. The day arrived, the family arrived, the goose was sizzling in the oven and the chef was in a good mood and confident of victory despite his multiple roles as chef, waiter and entertainer. Potatoes in the pot, vegetables in the pan, a sauce conjured up from the gravy, finally the goose carved, and everything served. There was applause and relief. But the result was disillusioning. The goose meat had retained an astonishing firmness and the sauce floated helplessly around on the plate. Unfortunately, the cook had also forgotten to put the pot with the potatoes on the stove, so they stood cold and raw in the kitchen. The family took it all in their stride, and it remained a harmonious Christmas Day together.

The old lady's personal hygiene continued to decline and required constant reminders and help. Her loneliness also required me to check on her several times a day, if only to make sure she didn't develop too many strange ideas of her own. All of this became a huge challenge alongside my studies and the necessary part-time jobs. We managed it together for a while, but it became increasingly difficult as her dementia progressed. If she then also did her big business next to the toilet instead of in the toilet, that was a particular challenge even for a medical student. But when she also started to leave the house and wander the streets, at some point it just wasn't possible anymore. With a heavy heart, I had to put her in a care home. It wasn't a good experience, and I would have liked to have spared her that. But I couldn't see any other option. Grandma Mathilde didn't last long in this care home. She died there in 1981.

Is it right to stay in your own four walls until you really can't go on? Only to then be rushed into the next available care bed? And to wait there, lonely and lost, for death because you are no longer able to adapt to a new environment?

My landlord was deeply saddened by the infirmity and the silent, lonely death of his grandmother Mathilde in the anonymity of this shabby nursing home. He blamed himself for not having reacted sooner. With careful planning, a friendlier care home could have been found earlier. But would everyone have understood? Or would there perhaps have been accusations that he had pushed Grandma away to have the house to himself? He couldn't stop thinking about how the last stage of his life could be better organized. This would play an important role in his own thoughts and decisions much later.

The Big Renovation

I was now alone in the house. Grandmother Mathilde had left it to me. But the house, which had been used for years, was now in need of care and renovation. For a house with outdated technology in need of renovation and a student with limited financial resources, a way had to be found to carry out the necessary repairs.

In fact, I found myself in a poor state. Not only were practically all the rooms in need of major renovation, if only to remove the colorful wallpaper, which was now considered impossible. The infrastructure also left a lot to be desired. The old oil-fired heating system (which used to run on coal in earlier times) via hot air ducts only supplied the ground floor and first floor anyway ~ and that was quite inadequate, at least on the upper floor. The two rooms on the top floor were heated by an electric radiator. The old wooden windows with their small casements were already quite leaky and you could feel the draught in the room when it was windy. There was no central hot water supply. The old, enameled bathtub on four legs with a hand shower was supplied with hot water by an electric instantaneous water heater. An instantaneous water heater also supplied the sink in the kitchen. The floors were a disaster. The linoleum in the hallway was scratched and dull. The wooden floors on the upper floor, in the stairwell and in the attic, which were painted with "oxblood" at the time, competed in their timeless ugliness with the terrazzo floors in the kitchen, bathroom and guest toilet. Carpets, where present, were worn and no longer really clean. And finally, the roof had been in need of renovation for a long time. The garden was also overgrown and the weeds had long since taken over. The lawn was more like a meadow with lots of "dandelions" ~ much to the constant annoyance of the neighbors.

If all these defects had been professionally rectified, it would have cost a small fortune - unthinkable in my financial situation as a student with a small additional income. Nevertheless, a period of renovation began for the house - with unexpected help from various sources.

Friends were found to lend a hand. First and foremost, Schufti, who had a different name but wanted to be called that. And he lived up to his name - he could really work hard. Schufti is big and strong and could work for hours with a BoschHammer that I had borrowed for the renovation work. Our first project in 1980 was a wall breakthrough between the two large rooms on the ground floor. Two rooms were to become one. As the building plan had specified that a steel girder was to be inserted crosswise at this point, the opening was planned to be two meters wide. However, this steel girder was not present, and no steel could be found in the wall, even with test drillings and a magnetic detector. So, we reduced our breakthrough plan to a width of one meter, as it was a load-bearing wall after all. For additional stability, we added a round arch to the top of the breakthrough. Schufti managed this with astonishing precision using his heavy equipment.

Once the equipment was in place and the rubble was already piling up, we immediately tackled a second project: cutting slots to lay pipes for a central heating system. This was tedious and spread the rubble all over the house. The pipes were then laid by a plumber, who also installed a new gas heating system. Now the house had central heating! After removing the considerable amount of rubble, we also carried out the necessary wallpapering and painting work in the most important rooms. The bathroom received a new, monstrous blue bathtub made of Plexiglass. The house shone in new splendor and new warmth.

I nominate Schufti as a "hero of the house". Without his friendly work, these necessary and important changes and renovations would not have happened so soon. Schufti was a stroke of luck for me, I was on a real winning streak, because more strokes of luck were to follow.

With the new heating system, the planned budget and my bank account were already well overdrawn. And the urgently needed renovation of the leaking windows was still pending. Unexpectedly, support came from two sides that no one had previously planned for. The airport offered residents in a newly established noise protection zone subsidies for soundproof windows. A glance at the map showed that the boundary of this noise protection zone ran right through my property. It took a few applications, a negotiation, an expert opinion - and then the funding approval was on the table. At the same time, the city was running a program to improve thermal insulation in old buildings. Here, too, the planned new windows met all the requirements for a corresponding subsidy. Both grants together covered all but a small amount of the costs for installing new sound and heat-insulating windows. I opted for aluminum windows with wide double glazing and a sound insulation value of 42 decibels. The windows were to be brown to match the color of the walls. However, the custom-made windows were then supplied in black, which brought the price again down a little. My bank account and I could breathe a sigh of relief. But any further repairs would have to wait.

A Secret Night of Love

Like a good ghost from the past, Ursula has popped up from time to time in recent years. Ursula was my first steady girlfriend during my late school days at the Gymnasium Köln-Deutz. Hours of phone calls and meetings or parties at the weekend, which we laboriously arranged with our parents, were our program. I'll never forget the first big kiss at a school party in an old tower of the Cologne city wall, a unique feeling of happiness that was completely unknown to both of us until then. Once we'd acquired a taste for it, after our harmless Saturday night pleasures, there was no evening walk home without regular breaks for more kisses. Most of the time, when I took Ursula home, we even got off the streetcar one stop earlier to have a longer walk along the Rhine. We lived and loved these moments of happiness, perhaps also as compensation for some domestic problems. I was sure of the fuss when I came home late because of it. We didn't care about the reactions of passers-by. There was nothing more than that and a few cautious touches. With the given domestic circumstances and the strict supervision of the parents, there was practically no opportunity for any kind of more intimate togetherness. And with our inherited inhibitions, we would hardly have dared to take up Christoph's mother's generous offer concerning the guest room.

I didn't get on well with Ursula's parents either. They didn't like me very much and I didn't like them at all. Maybe I let it show too much. The relationship between my parents and Ursula's parents also remained very distant, which became apparent at a dance school prom. Due to pressure from her parents and my approaching A-levels, our meetings became less frequent. When I moved to Aachen to start university the day after my Abitur, we lost sight of each other. Although Ursula also moved to Aachen two years later to study, we had both made new friends in the meantime. However, nothing had changed in my feelings for Ursula. Our encounters remained cordial, but ultimately non-binding. And so, it always hurt me that she seemed to feel more comfortable in the company of others - with all the consequences. It hit me in the heart when I knew she was sleeping with others. The howling misery came at night, when the tension of the exhausting study day subsided. I would have loved to win her back for myself. But I couldn't change anything because my own situation was desolate. I was stretched to my limits trying to complete my engineering degree, which was not exactly easy. Then there was the chronic lack of money. The budget Dad gave me wasn't really enough for a decent student flat and a decent diet. I couldn't show my shabby place to anyone, no way to a girlfriend. The tiny room in the backyard with a small sink and a shared toilet barely allowed for the most basic hygiene. Going out with my girlfriend was out of the question. Other fellow students were more flexible, and a colleague from a higher semester took a liking to my school friend and managed to win her over. They got married soon afterwards, and I sadly watched the wedding from a back corner of the church. Ursula then moved to southern Germany with her husband. After a while, I was also married to Brigitte. That didn't change the inner bond between Ursula and me. Even after that, there were further meetings, which we had carefully planned and arranged, usually four of us with our spouses. And we always looked for and found an opportunity for a big secret kiss that rekindled the old feelings. For example, on a joint excursion to the beautiful caves of Han/Belgium, where dark side passages of the cave away from the group offered themselves for a few little detours.

And so it was that one-day Ursula, now a doctor and mother of two, came by for a coffee. She had just spent a few days with her parents in Cologne and was looking forward to the visit to Düsseldorf and the reunion. She didn't know that I had broken up with Brigitte again in the meantime. We had so much to talk about and exchange: How could we have lost sight of each other like that? What happened during the time we were apart? What about our feelings for each other? Why didn't we find each other again? It was getting late.

Ursula stayed the night. The waiting guest room was not an issue. As if it had never been any different, we prepared to spend the night together. It was our night, the first and only one. The mutual desire that had built up over so many years and had so often been suppressed erupted in an explosion of emotions when we first touched. It was a night full of love, happiness and passion. Tears also flowed, as we both knew that there could be no going back and no going forward, only the here and now. Sleep was out of the question; every minute was too precious. Many past situations emerged from our memories and demanded that we catch up on what we had missed back then. It was only that night that we realized what we had really felt for each other over the years - a great love that we had somehow simply missed. We were finally able to experience for a brief moment what had been suppressed for so long. The fear of letting go came with the dawn, which we saw through the small window with mixed feelings, happy, exhausted, but also with the sad certainty that our night was coming to an end. At breakfast, we were brought back to reality by an urgent phone call from worried parents who had already missed her. When Ursula finally had to leave, the farewell was long and painful. Every last kiss was followed by another and another. It was raining and even the house seemed to be crying when her car finally disappeared around the next bend.

We met a few more times over the next few years in a professional context at conferences and congresses. There was never another night. Ursula died of cancer in July 2013.

As a house, you can experience great theater sometimes. Two people are caught up in their past. They realize that they have missed out on something big together and at the same time that this train has long since departed and cannot be caught. For a few hours, they ride a rollercoaster of emotions, shared happiness, sadness about what they missed out on and the simple realization of reality. Material for a play, a drama. Life does not always follow your own wishes and decisions. In the variety of possibilities, it often finds a different path. The question is always tempting: what if ...? If they had found each other much earlier in the security of a home? Nobody knows. With hindsight, we can only say that they both found happiness independently of each other. However, one last uncertainty was finally resolved during their night together. For so many years, they had both enjoyed their little happiness again and again, without really communicating the great feelings that had probably existed for a long time. On this night, their great mutual love was experienced and expressed together for the first time, and the last unanswered question was thus answered and closed. The final statement was given by death.

Beautiful Second Study

In the winter semester of 1976, I began my second study, medicine, in Düsseldorf. It was so different from the hard and, at least initially, hardship-filled engineering course in Aachen. I now had a house, a small lime green

BMW and a fairly regular, albeit modest income. I quickly made friends among my fellow students and found a study group to help me prepare for the frequent exams. My problems tended to lie outside of university life: the crucial phase of separating from Brigitte, looking after my elderly and increasingly demented grandmother Mathilde, running the household and balancing my job and studies. Things got a bit hectic at times. But it was worth it, for my dream course of study, for the wonderful working group with Marlies and Annedore and for many other dear friends such as Marion, Rainer, Maria, Eleonore, Isa and others. And especially Barbara, but more on that later.

But my professional activities also had their exiting sides during this time. My main job as managing director of an environmental association occasionally took me to England and France to contact international partner organizations. As long as I still had long hair, I even had a favorite hairdresser in London. There I would have a whisky before my haircut to relieve the tension before the necessary action. But what I enjoyed most of all: I was also a part-time physics teacher at a grammar school.

I don't think he was a bad teacher. He wanted to convey as much of physics as possible to the pupils through experiments that he had carefully prepared at home. There were small explosions in the classroom, an implosion in the schoolyard by blowing up a television tube and the launch of a water rocket. The speed of light, the speed of sound and the rotation of the earth were demonstrated experimentally and made measurable. Even his black and white cat was included to show how and why she always falls on its feet. The pupils also enthusiastically took part in a research project on noise control. They used firecrackers and microphones to investigate the reverberation of urban canyons. When a streetcar driver who was observing what was happening refused to drive on, my teacher arrived home quite exhausted after fleeing the measurement site. But his theoretical lectures on "Cybernetics" and "Theory of Relativity" for elective students also required many hours of intensive preparation at home.

In between, there was also a nursing internship during the semester break. That was quite a challenge for me, who had little to do with illness, hospitals and nursing apart from my first experiences with Grandma Mathilde. I found the concentrated geriatrics of a male internal medicine ward with its fates, sounds and smells overwhelming. I was allowed to mop up various excrements from the floor and accompany dying patients in their final hours. I was able to learn a lot from the excellent Korean ward headnurse but was mocked as a "luxury student" because of my lime green BMW. As a result, I often had to take on the more unpleasant tasks. All this made me doubt in the early days whether my decision to go into medicine was really the right one. The engineering profession was certainly less upsetting in this respect. But this phase also passed, and I still had the feeling that I had gained important experience for my future career as a doctor.

A beautiful friendship developed with Annedore and Marlies that went beyond the working group. We also took it easy at work. We usually spent an hour chatting over an Irish coffee before we threw ourselves into the catalogs with the thousands of exam questions. As I was traveling a lot due to grandma and work, I regularly brought up the rear in the study group. The fact that the other two bravely pulled me through anyway probably made it possible for me to study medicine smoothly and without any delays. I am still very grateful to both of them today.

I would also have liked to have given this wonderful study group space. There was plenty of space, and as far as I know, there was usually enough whisky for an Irish coffee in the bar. But I'm on the other side of town and the other two would have had to travel a long way. Besides, my student was usually on his way to university in his lime green BMW anyway. So, the study group usually met at Annedore's, because she also had a large dining table and whisky in the house (which my student also occasionally bought supplies for).

Studying and Love

What would student life be without love? With so many like-minded people and peers who see each other almost every day, loving encounters are to be expected. However, the encounter with my first "chosen one", Maria, did not lead to the relationship I had hoped for.

When I expressed my interest to her after a few meetings, she told me that she was already taken. Obviously, she had made the right choice, because they are still together today!

Barbara studied medicine in the same semester, but also psychology at the same time. She wasn't directly part of our working group with Annedore and Marlies but was often with us. Barbara lived in a small room in the private house of an elderly lady. She was a clever and very ambitious student and - unlike me - had even understood the difficult biochemistry lecture quite well. We liked each other right from the start. So, it was only natural that I asked her to explain biochemistry to me so that I wouldn't embarrass myself even more in front of my working group. However, when it came to the first "tutoring session" and we were sitting on her bed with our lecture notes due to lack of space, we discovered that we had feelings and wishes in common that went far beyond the subject of biochemistry. There was no more room on the bed for the documents. Barbara had suffered a difficult fate: Her first boyfriend was killed in a car accident and she herself was seriously injured. And I was still gnawing at my self-doubt and self-reproach because of my divorce. In addition to coming to terms with the past together, we developed a very loving relationship. We were a couple for a few years and had a great time during my studies. When I was drawn to South America again during this time, she drove to Paris in her old Beetle to pick me up at the airport on the way back on my cheap flight. And then she drove me straight back to Düsseldorf. Her landlady just shook her head at this feat.

Barbara was a doer, and she showed that in her studies too. She completed her two-degree courses in parallel within the minimum period of study. For her later career, she chose psychiatry, maybe one of the most difficult areas of medicine. In her specialty, geriatric psychiatry, she later became probably the most prominent expert in the Düsseldorf area with her numerous projects and activities.

I also held Barbara in high esteem! Although she didn't live within my walls, she was a frequent and welcome guest. When she was there, she lent a hand. She had a keen eye for what needed to be done and usually wanted to get it done straight away. I was happy for my landlord about this beautiful and harmonious relationship and could well have imagined that it would become something permanent. Unfortunately, things turned out differently.

Everything was going well in our relationship, we were in love and happy together, had common interests and wonderful experiences. Until one day Barbara came over with an important question. She wanted clarity about the further development of our relationship, which would soon lead to a marriage with children after we had finished our studies. Barbara wanted a binding decision about our plans before we had even finished our studies. Unfortunately, we were unable to reach an agreement on this important issue. I myself was not yet in a position to make such a decision. I was far too busy dealing with the aftermath of my divorce, with some South American dreams and illusions, also with a vague fear of bringing children into the world. All of this made it impossible for me to draw up a concrete life plan together. As a result, Barbara consequently ended the relationship. In another partner, she found someone who shared her concrete wishes and ideas for the near future. Never before - and never again - has someone so clearly and decisively "kicked me out". It was painful to simply finish what we had experienced and achieved together, but we managed to part in great friendship. The couple was history, but the friendship and bond remained.

They managed that quite well! Different time horizons led to life plans that were difficult to reconcile. Discussions brought clarity and the bitter consequence without giving up completely what they had in common. As a house, I am in the fortunate position of never having experienced a real "war of the roses" within my walls. Separations yes, even a divorce, but shouting and flying household objects are alien to me. I've heard completely different stories from other houses. You could learn from this: the chair put in front of the door doesn't necessarily mean that your feelings are also sitting there. Or to put it another way: you can't just throw love out the door.

Party Time

With the relaxed atmosphere of the second study and the separation finally over, the desire to party also grew. And the big house naturally offered ideal conditions for this. My 30th birthday in 1978 marked the start of a series of four legendary events in my house. More than 75 people came to the first party, I soon lost track of the exact number. Fellow students, childhood friends, current friends, former work colleagues, my pupils from secondary school and probably a few guests they had brought with them followed the invitation. There was lots of bread, half a loaf of fresh Gouda cheese, a good hundred sausages, a few salads the guests had brought along, a large barrel of beer and a few bottles of red wine. All three floors and the stairs were occupied, and there was loud music for dancing at the top floor. The "bear was raging" and the house was shaking. For the steadfast, there was coffee in the morning and leftovers from the evening for breakfast.

I have to emphatically reject that; my thick outer walls didn't shake! As far as the interior construction was concerned, the statics of the ceilings and the stairs were certainly at their limits. But what the heck, nothing broke or flaked off. The full extent of the mess and devastation only became apparent when calm returned in the late morning. And the landlord and a few hard-working helpers set about dumping the garbage into large bin bags and putting everything back in its proper place. I survived this first big ordeal of the party unscathed – but there were more to come.

It continued the very next year, with a similar line-up and a similar schedule. This time on February 10, in other words "to get me in the mood and start into my birthday on February 11". At midnight, there were sparklers, a toast with a speech and lots of applause when the presents were unwrapped.

I had become accustomed to the stress level by now. But the number of sparklers that were lit at the same time did worry me a little. After all, most of my floors and stairs are made of wood and there are lots of other flammable things lying around. A fireman's hair would have stood on end. Luckily there was no one there, he would have had to stop everything immediately, and the feared fire didn't happen. Nevertheless, I didn't feel well again within my walls until the next morning after the cleaning crew and lots of garbage bags had been put to good use.

1980 was the year of major alterations and renovations in the house, so it wasn't until 1981 that we celebrated my 33rd birthday again. And so, it continued in the usual way. At the beginning, I symbolically cut a ribbon in honor of Schufti in the passageway he had so meticulously created between the living and dining room and gave a short speech. After that, it was business as usual. It was a party.

In 1982, I had a party with Gitte, a mutual friend from the early days of my marriage to Brigitte. Gitte's birthday was on February 15, just a few days after mine. We decided to celebrate her birthday on February 14 with a joint party. The theme was "Dance of the Vampires". Appropriate costumes were requested. Scary images and scenes played out on the street as the guests arrived punctually at 10 pm. Inside, gruesome and "bloody" rituals were celebrated, red fire punch was served, apparently blood-smeared figures danced waltzes and recited scary stories. Shortly before midnight, two burly men carried in a crate. There was champagne for everyone and at the stroke of midnight the box was opened, and Gitte was freed from her "coffin". She thanked the other vampires with a speech and was then allowed to unwrap her presents. Afterwards, everyone was served red "blood soup" and music from "The Rocky Horror Show".

With just 30 guests, this last party was the least stressful for me. The chaos the next morning was also limited and quickly cleared up. However, I thought I noticed a certain amount of irritation in the neighboring houses about the "bloody" event with the strange characters...

Exam Stress and a New Housemate

My fellow student Isa was short and had long, wavy brown hair. We liked each other straight away but had little contact. I only knew that her visible walking disability was due to her illness, multiple sclerosis. Rather by chance, I found out that she urgently needed a new apartment. Even then, it wasn't easy to find an apartment in Düsseldorf that was affordable for a student. As I was living alone in my house at the time, I offered her the chance to move into a room of my house. She gladly accepted, and the house soon had a new resident. She got the corner room on the second floor, perhaps the nicest room in the house, which until then I had only occasionally used as a second living room to watch TV. I didn't ask her for rent, she just had to pay for a new carpet that she wanted herself. Isa was a very quiet and pleasant housemate. Using the communal areas, kitchen and bathroom, was also no problem with her. We didn't have a close relationship, but we got on well.

I was traveling a lot during this time anyway. The first state examination lay ahead of us, a huge amount of material from all clinical subjects. This required regular and intensive meetings of our small working group. And, of course, appropriate preparation, which I had to do in a quiet corner at home. The exam was a great challenge for all three of us, although I was probably the weakest member of the group due to my limited previous medical knowledge and my part-time professional activities. Annedore was the strongest and the driving force of the group, so to speak, she simply pulled us along.

The day of the exam came in March 1981. Marlies suffered from exam anxiety, a problem that I fortunately never had. At the start of an exam, I'm as cold and calm as an iceberg. After the exam we had to wait about a week for the result. Then the shock: Marlies had failed, a year was lost for her. I had passed, not particularly well, but sufficiently. Annedore had done very well, as expected.

A Korean Temptation

I met So-Ra* in 1981 during my practical year at Krefeld Hospital in the operating theater. I had chosen anesthesia as an elective subject and was allowed to induce anesthesia and monitor patients during surgery under supervision. So-Ra worked as an anesthesia nurse in this area and so I was able to learn a lot from her experience. I didn't see much of her face at work, it mostly disappeared behind the large mask. This and her Asian background made her somehow mysterious and interesting to me. Curious, I approached her once after work and managed to get her to go on a date. Like many others, So-Ra had come to Germany from Korea as a nurse. But her real passion was ceramics. So, alongside her work as a nurse anesthetist, she began to study ceramic design at Krefeld University of Applied Sciences. We had a nice evening in a restaurant in Düsseldorf, after which she wanted to see my house. There was a lot to talk about, Korea was still a completely unknown country for me. And So-Ra knew a lot of beautiful and exciting things to talk about it - she

*Name changed

just didn't talk much about her family. But she wanted to know even more about my surroundings. At midnight, I offered her the option of staying on or taking her home now. So-Ra hesitantly chose to go home at first, wrestled with herself for a moment and then made her decision. She stayed.

The mood, the topics, the sympathy, the mutual interest - everything was right from the start. The decision had been made and we could see the anticipation of what was to come in each other's eyes. We enjoyed our first curious and loving sex and the night together to the full. Everything was wonderful and we made lots of plans for further meetings over breakfast. It was clear that we wanted to stay together. I don't think I've ever fallen in love so quickly. But So-Ra didn't live with me. She kept her room in a student hall of residence in Krefeld. But she was often here, her old Citroen made commuting the short distance easy.

When I visited her in Krefeld, things usually happened very quickly. The mutual desire was always great; waiting and drinking tea first was not our strong point. Her light summer dress often slipped to the floor as soon as I kissed her hello. "You've been here less than two minutes and I'm already wearing nothing," she would protest, laughing. Only to actively show her agreement and joy at the same time. We were happy together.

We were a couple for about three years and had many wonderful experiences together. I will never forget a trip to Montreux for the Medica with a few nights in an old hotel on a hill on the outskirts of the city. The house looked like a somewhat dilapidated castle to us, but from the terrace of our room we had a wonderful view of Lake Geneva. After our daily congress visits, we sat on the large, secluded terrace late into the night, enjoying our love and the warm summer air and dreaming of a future together.

It was obvious and therefore not hidden from me either: So-Ra succeeded in freeing my landlord from deep-seated inhibitions from his youth and also from self-reproach because of his divorce. In the close and strict parental home, contact with girls was viewed rather critically and hindered. This left its mark, also on his self-image. With her love and her fresh, natural sexuality, So-Ra managed to untangle this knot. You could see my landlord's new joy of life!

So-Ra is a gifted ceramic artist. She makes beautiful vessels, vases, plates and bowls, many of which are still in my house today. However, there also was a big problem in our relationship, and that was her pathological jealousy. It didn't take long for Isa to succumb to it. So-Ra ultimately demanded that she move out of my house. The argument dragged on for a while until Isa finally gave up in exasperation and looked for a new place to live. So-Ra meticulously researched my past, and she was always suspicious of my existing friendships. Once, when my former fellow student Maria, now already married, came to visit me and we said goodbye at the front door with a friendly kiss, she made a terrible scene in the street. Something like that led to days of resentment. The relationship became more difficult. On good days, we thought about setting up a workshop with a kiln for her ceramic work in my basement. On bad days, she sometimes didn't say a word. She never really warmed to my family and friends either, her constant mistrust was a barrier. She got into a big fight with the neighbors over a few raspberries that they had picked in our absence so that they wouldn't spoil. We ended our relationship several times, only to start again after some time and many apologies. There was a lot of love between us, despite all the problems, but the relationship couldn't have a future like that.

It could have been so beautiful. I would have loved having the ceramics workshop of a renowned artist within my walls just as much as the landlord. It's a shame that things turned out differently. Jealousy cannot be explained rationally, it is like a disease that gnaws away at important vital functions. So-Ra was later awarded a professorship at a university in Seoul for her work, also she received several awards in Germany.

Assistant Doctor with a Monster Car

I found my first paid job as an assistant doctor on the men's internal medicine ward of the Catholic St. Marien Hospital in Ratingen from August 1, 1982. As I had left the Protestant church many years ago and was therefore non-denominational, the head doctor implored me to keep this fact a secret from colleagues and patients. The medical responsibility for thirty to forty patients was a very demanding task - even under the supervision of a senior physician and the head physician. It required full commitment, usually over and above regular working hours. In addition, there were around ten night-shifts per month, several of them 24 hours at the weekend. Due to the many shifts, the pay for this job was very satisfactory, so I was able to fulfill a few extra wishes for the first time in a long time. Now, I wanted a bigger car. Following my preference for American cars, I found an older Chevrolet Monte Carlo that wasn't all that expensive. The five-metre-long coupé only had two doors and four seats, but an eight-cylinder engine with a capacity of five liters. I only realized later how much petrol this car monster swallowed. The neighbors reacted to the colossus on my doorstep with meaningful silence, the head doctor with mild derision. But I had fun, even though the car had a life of its own and the engine often only wanted to start after a lot of persuasion.

During this time, I also got to know Cecilia, the idolized Filipino ward headnurse on the internal medicine women's ward, who was always careful to keep her admirers at a distance. There was no touching or close contact with her - a rather unusual attitude in the Catholic hospital. Cecilia was married and soon expecting Abdon, her first and only child. The sight of her with her big pregnant belly gracefully pushing the trolley through the ward was not only pleasing to me. Cecilia was a popular and respected figure in the hospital. We became friends and grew closer over time, so that I also found out about her difficult marriage. But little did I know at the time that this would change my life in unexpected and profound ways.

Cecilia's first direct contact with my Monte Carlo, which she also wanted to drive once, was less fortunate. In order to drive off, she had to back up a bit, but hadn't realized that the steering was fully engaged, and the front wheels were pointing to the left. So, nothing moved at first, because the front wheels touched the kerb. Then Cecilia stepped on the gas, a lot of gas, and the eight-cylinder engine showed what it was capable of. The car shot diagonally backwards and crashed into the side of my neighbor's car, a brand-new VW Passat, which was parked opposite. Both side doors were dented, only the Monte Carlo was "unimpressed". So, I was in for an unpleasant visit to my neighbor, who responded in a very friendly and calm manner. "I don't see any damage," he said after looking out of the front door. When I showed him around his car, he did turn a little pale.

Magic Encounter at Machu Picchu

In the middle of my somewhat complicated relationship world at the time, Teresa paid me a visit. I had invited her myself. I met Teresa on July 28, 1978, on my first trip to Peru on the train from Cuzco to Machu Picchu. She sat next to me, and we got talking, a curious mutual acquaintance. Teresa is 13 years younger than me; she had just turned 18 at the time. She was on her first trip to Cuzco and Machu Picchu with her aunt and some other relatives, something like a must for every Peruvian. After all, Machu Picchu was the religious and cultural center of the Incas, the proud South American civilization with its most important sites in what is now Peru. Even today, Machu Picchu is still a magical place whose spiritual power is hard to escape, even though thousands of tourists trample over the historic stones every day. I managed to walk through the once sacred city alone with Teresa. We had successfully separated ourselves from her family. The magic of this extraordinary place quickly captivated us both. I took her hand to help her climb to a high step and never let go. At the altar, whose touch promises lifelong blessings and eternal friendship, we accepted this promise together with a fleeting embrace. Much later, I found out that she had waited for a kiss. I must have missed this opportunity; I just didn't have the courage. On the way back to Cusco, again with her family, and in the evening in the city, we had plenty of time to talk and get to know each other better. We stayed in touch afterwards, initially only with occasional letters. But on a second trip to Peru, I visited Teresa for the first time at home in Chiclayo, in the north of Peru. Later, I was also able to spend Christmas with her family - in the Peruvian summer and on the beach, a very special experience. When we started sending emails, the constant contact intensified. Teresa had never been abroad before, and I realized that it was her great wish to come to Europe one day. In 1983, I invited her to visit me in Germany and spend three weeks with me. She gladly accepted, and so her first trip abroad could begin in September 1983.

A Visit with Conflicts

At that time, I was in a constant ON-OFF relationship with my girlfriend So-Ra. When I invited Teresa, we were just in the deepest OFF state. But when So-Ra found out about the invitation, she did everything in her power to get the relationship back to ON - and she was successful. Although Teresa had not come with the intention of starting a close relationship with me, So-Ra's legendary jealousy meant that conflicts were inevitable. And that's what happened.

Actually, it could have been a wonderful understanding between three people from three continents. But So-Ra was hostile towards Teresa right from the start. Teresa, for her part, had a very positive attitude to life and was generally able to deal with it quite well, even if it sometimes became difficult. She lived in the small guest room on the second floor and actively helped out in the household from the very beginning. I learned why this is worth mentioning a little later during another visit from Peru.

We went on several trips in my old Monte Carlo, to the surrounding area, to Cologne, to Dad and Gerd, to Amsterdam and even to Switzerland. Teresa always had to sit in the back of the car, while So-Ra wouldn't let anyone take her place in the front. Despite the constant tension, we also had wonderful experiences together at home and on the road. But a few days before Teresa's departure, the conflicts became more and more intense. So-Ra left the house again and the relationship went back to OFF. I spent the last few days alone with Teresa, it was a rest for both of us. Teresa also got to know Cecilia during these days. While shopping together at the supermarket, Teresa confided her impression of So-Ra to her: "She's a devil!"

But for Teresa and me, the mysterious magic of Machu Picchu continued to work. We often had the same thoughts and, in many ways, the same feelings and attitudes. Teresa has remained a good and loyal friend to me. We are still in regular contact via email, social media and occasional visits to Peru. In 2019, she visited Düsseldorf again as part of a trip to Europe.

A Lecture Tour with Consequences

On my first trip to Peru in 1978, I also met Maria and Grace, two friends and fellow students who were studying law at the University of Arequipa. They looked out of the window from the university next to the Plaza de Armas and were amused by me as a tourist. I stood in front of the magnificent gate and tried to find out what kind of building it was. But they were curious enough to ask me where I was from. I bought them coffee and ice cream in the plaza, we got talking and eventually arranged to go on a trip to an old mill nearby the next afternoon. Grace was the spokesperson and Maria was the quiet one, she didn't speak any English either. But I liked her, with her brown skin and long black hair. Maria came from Tacna, the southernmost city in Peru, close to the Chilean border, a rather dreamy little town. Arequipa, also in southern Peru, with its university, is the nearest larger city. I stayed in touch with Maria even after our meeting. We wrote letters to each other and met up occasionally on my next trips. Once I also visited her in her hometown of Tacna. Of course, I was also interested in her law studies, as there are some interesting differences between the Peruvian and German legal systems. In a burst of arrogance, not to say megalomania, I had agreed to give a lecture on environmental law in Germany at her university during one of my later visits to Arequipa - a real challenge given my marginal knowledge of Spanish. Of course, this promise had to be kept.

As I didn't want to travel to South America just to give a lecture, I planned a long detour to Arequipa. This took me from Manaus/Brazil via Rio de Janeiro, Sao Paulo, the Igacu waterfalls, Buenos Aires/Argentina and La Paz/Bolivia to Puno/Peru. From there, I took a packed collectivo to Arequipa, partly on gravel roads. After this adventurous journey, I arrived at my hotel in the Plaza de Armas the day before my lecture, completely dusty. After a thorough dusting and cleaning, the lecture could take place the next day. I had completed the manuscript with the help of the lawyers from my environmental association and a Spanish-speaking friend. The reception by the Dean of the Faculty of Law was dignified and the auditorium listened to my presentation with polite interest and a slight smile at my accent. The subsequent discussion was held in English thanks to Grace's translations. Afterwards there was champagne from the dean in the circle of lecturers. Maria and Grace proudly enjoyed their fame as mediator and translator.

I could well imagine a closer relationship with Maria. In Arequipa and Tacna, there had already been some lovely kisses, even in the presence of her family. Maybe that's why she accepted my invitation to Germany in 1985, despite her mother's expressed (but not necessarily serious) reservations. It turned out to be a disaster.

He hinted at it himself, so I may as well anticipate a little. There were plenty of problems with his two lavish invitations from Peruvian girlfriends here in Germany. The first time, with Teresa, it was the jealous girlfriend So-Ra who repeatedly prevented a pleasant stay together. The host's idea of a harmonious trio from three continents proved to be rather naive in this case. The second time, with Maria, it was the invitee herself who made a pleasant stay almost impossible, as we will see in a moment.

But if you ask the host, he will tell you that despite all the problems, there were also some wonderful experiences together. And that for this reason, and because of the learnings he had with the visits, the invitations were definitely worthwhile for him. Teresa later came ma second time for a much more harmonious visit.

Another Difficult Visit

Everything had to be beautiful, the house had to shine. A week before Maria's arrival, I decided to "quickly" renovate the staircase. But the old wallpaper didn't stand up to the paint, it came loose and had to be replaced. Wallpapering in a high stairwell - a real challenge. In any case, it wasn't easy to do overnight, even if you were prepared to work at night. The final coat of paint was applied on the last day before Maria's arrival, with cleaning and tidying up done at night. In the morning, I went to Frankfurt Airport by car.

I have rarely seen the landlord so hectic. He hadn't found anyone in a hurry to help him with the work that needed doing. When the old wallpaper above the stairs came off while he was trying to repaint it, the disaster was complete. The ceiling height at this point is around four meters, and it is difficult to get a ladder to stand securely on the stairs. Nevertheless, he finally managed to put up the new wallpaper. Of course I was delighted with the renovation, but I was also a little worried about the landlord when I thought about the work, some of which was carried out at night and not without danger. And then the stress wasn't even worth it ...

After the joyful welcome at the airport, the first reality check came quickly: the incredulous look at my little car and the unmistakable disappointment at the missing Mercedes star. The gas-guzzling Monte Carlo was long gone and there was now a little runabout, a white Peugeot 205 GTI, on my doorstep. This was not the limousine that Maria would have wanted for her reception. When we arrived home, she was in for another shock: the welcome she had expected to receive from the spirits on duty didn't materialize. Maria couldn't understand why I was living alone in this house without any servants. She didn't come from a very wealthy family either, but domestic help was a matter of course in her house. My own cooking skills at our first dinner together didn't really convince her either. On the other hand, she wasn't prepared to help me with the housework in any way either. Maria was pursuing her own dream: a luxurious life as a princess in Germany without financial or other restrictions. This dream could only be disappointed in a bachelor household like mine. Princess Maria wanted to be served and not be involved in any way in a shared household. When I once had to carry a washing machine out of the cellar, I had to heave the bulky appliance up the cellar stairs on my own without my friend lending a helping hand. Her relationship with my family and friends remained rather reserved during several visits due to her lack of English skills, but also because of her demeanor. Our relationship also became increasingly cool, and a closer relationship could no longer develop.

For me, the course of this visit, which I had expected a lot from, was a great disappointment. The farewell in Frankfurt was friendly, but already very distant. I met Maria again later in Peru, but the estrangement was irreversible. The Peruvian beauty had successfully destroyed our dream herself with her airs and graces - a dream that we obviously perceived and interpreted very differently.

She didn't like me - and I didn't like her either. She had probably hoped that the landlord would present her a magnificent villa with lots of servants and a luxury limousine outside the door. That could only lead to great disappointment, for her, but also for me. What I urgently needed at the time were helping hands to tidy up, clean and renovate. I, the house, could do nothing with an idle princess. Even various cleaning assistants that the landlord had hired in the meantime were unable to cope satisfactorily with the work at hand. But improvement was in sight...

Above the Clouds

My work at the hospital was quite strenuous because of the many shifts and countless hours of overtime, but also because of the great responsibility we residents were given. To compensate, I decided to take up a rather expensive hobby and fulfill an old dream: I wanted to get my pilot's license. My research led me to a flying school in Essen where you could get your license in evening classes on the side. You could also charter planes there, as owning my own plane was far beyond my financial means. Just obtaining the license and the necessary lessons and flying hours were time-consuming and quite expensive. Then, on September 1, 1984, came the long-awaited first solo flight in a Cessna 152, a truly exciting experience. The test flight followed soon after. First, I flew solo with the larger Cessna 172 from Essen to Bonn-Hangelaer and from there with the examiner via several stops back to Hangelaer again. There I finally received the coveted flying license. This turned flying into an exciting hobby that not only gave me, but also my passengers, many new impressions and wonderful experiences over the following 15 years.

Daring to Try Something New

After almost four years, I had had enough of the hospital air. Although I had recently found a good intern position as a doctor in charge of the intensive care unit, I was looking for a change. An attractive offer as head of a medical service in a chemical company gave me the idea of being able to contribute my expertise as an engineer and doctor at the same time. I applied and was accepted. I started my new job on April 1, 1986. However, I needed an additional qualification in "occupational medicine". The new employer agreed to finance the three-month training course required for this at the beginning of my employment. The training center that offered a corresponding course for this period was in Berlin. So off I went to Berlin!

He disappeared to Berlin and once again left me here with my inadequate safeguards and without supervision - quite reckless from today's perspective. But he did come home more often at the weekend to check on things and do the necessary work. Incidentally, Berlin was by no means unknown to him...

Some time ago, I had met a Korean doctor in Berlin, Seo-Yong*, who offered to let me stay in her shared flat in Berlin whenever I wanted. Curious, I accepted her offer for a weekend.

There were about ten people living in this shared flat, almost all Koreans, in one of Berlin's typical very large apartments. They cooked together, I was allowed to take part in the meals and quickly took a liking to the group, the Korean cuisine - and to Seo-Yong. The table conversations were a colorful mix of Korean, German and English. I enjoyed coming to Berlin on a few more weekends. I shared her room with Seo-Yong - and her big mattress on the floor. Our relationship in this Korean and quite permissive shared flat environment was like a rush for me. Seo-Yong was a very exalted guy, quite shrill, loud, colorful, dazzling. But when you looked behind this crazy facade, a thoughtful, sensitive and very lovable woman emerged. In our obvious differences, we were already a striking couple. Yet our love affair was rather quiet and harmonious. I learned from her different way of life that you can do a lot

*name changed

of things differently - and some things simply better. Nevertheless, our very different "worlds" could hardly be united in the end. I wouldn't have been able to bring her into my world either. My family would certainly not have accepted her with her appearance. So, Seo-Yong never got to know my house. After a few wonderful and exciting weekends together, I ended the relationship.

Why is he telling us here about this rather brief affair, which also has nothing to do with me, the house? I think I know why. The relationship with Seo-Yong was short, but it changed him. He always came home from those weekends in Berlin very thoughtful. I think it was like an encounter with a completely different world for him. A world that was not compatible with his world in the long term, but which had broadened his perception of other ways of life, views and attitudes. My landlord became more relaxed, the Asian mentality became more familiar to him, and he began to appreciate it. And even after experiencing Korean jealousy before, he was now ready for the impending and final union with an Asian woman. But he couldn't know that yet.

So, when I started my industrial medicine training in Berlin, I didn't live with my Korean friend, but initially in a hotel. To my employer's delight, I quickly found a cheap, albeit far too big, apartment in Kreuzberg for short-term rental. It was a whole floor with several rooms and well over 100 square meters. A second-hand, but only partially functional television was also purchased for little money. I used the large apartment to invite as many friends as possible to Berlin. Many of them accepted the invitation, so the large apartment was used accordingly. The less demanding course left plenty of time for activities with friends. The degree was also no problem and so the requirements for my new job were met.

Back at home, unlike my work at the hospital, I now had regular working hours that allowed me to be home on time in the afternoons. With my little white runabout, I could usually get from home to work or back in about 25 minutes.

Cecilia

With the Peruvian dream of Maria shattered - and this was the good news in the disaster - another emerging problem had solved itself. A more intimate relationship with Maria would inevitably have come into conflict with the now inflamed love affair with Cecilia. But Cecilia was still married. That didn't stop us from appearing together at the subsequent family celebration in Düsseldorf's Rhine Tower when I finally had my doctorate in my pocket on May 16, 1986. Cecilia was very worried whether my family would accept her as a married woman with a child under these circumstances. To our mutual surprise, this concern turned out to be completely unfounded. On the contrary, she was warmly welcomed by both, Dad and Gerd, as my companion. Shortly afterwards, however, our relationship took an unexpected and dramatic turn.

The relationship with Cecilia was a ray of hope in my then busy but otherwise rather unsteady bachelor life. On November 20, 1986, I was sitting in my living room with Carmen, a nurse from our hospital. We had been to the movies and were now having a coffee and thinking about how the evening should continue. However, we no longer needed to make a decision. We hadn't expected it and hadn't realized that we weren't alone in the house. When we heard Cecilia calling from the second floor, I immediately realized that something serious must have happened. And so it was. Cecilia came downstairs and told us that she had left the house after another heated argument with her husband and didn't want to come back. Carmen quickly said goodbye. In the blink of an eye, a completely new situation had arisen. My house suddenly had a new resident. She came - and she stayed.

This initially caused a lot of trouble and suffering. Of course, Cecilia wanted custody of her son Abdon, who was just 7 years old at the time. But this failed due to the hard line taken by her husband's lawyer, who did not shy away from a smear campaign. Abdon stayed with his father and the prescribed contact between mother and son was ignored or torpedoed.

Cecilia immediately committed herself to her new home. She rolled up her sleeves and started tidying, cleaning and rearranging the furniture to make the house tidier and more homely.

She was very welcome from day one! Someone came into the house who looked after me and even my cellar. That hadn't happened for a long time! And it didn't stop at the cellar. After just a short time, I felt like having been cleaned and tidied from top to bottom. Household utensils that had not been used for decades, as well as cable remnants, dried wall paint and building materials in the cellar, long since buried under a thick layer of dust, went into the bin. Mysterious chemicals from Dad's chemical kitchen at home were carefully taken to the appropriate collection points. The floor and shelves, also freed from the layer of dust, shone in new cleanliness. The removal of the many boxes and cartons brought light and air into the musty cellar rooms. As I noticed, there were some discussions about the disposal of utensils that had not been used for a long time and still had a nostalgic value for the landlord. For the most part, however, a peaceful agreement was reached. The living rooms, although not quite as run-down as the cellar, underwent the same procedure. The beautiful large windows shone with a hitherto rather rare brilliance, and the floors also appeared rejuvenated. Even the carpet fringes now mostly pointed in one direction. The houseplants came to life, new ones were added and enjoyed a regular supply of water. The kitchen and bathroom were spotless, as far as the old fixtures and fittings allowed. In a word – I became presentable again.

Surprisingly, Cecilia took a liking to the old furniture in the house, some of which was very old, giving it a whole new lease of life. But even that couldn't prevent the ravages of time from continuing to gnaw away at the old pieces. When a friend wanted to spend the night with us and we put him up in my great-grandparents' double bed in the guest room, there was a loud bang in the room shortly after he went to bed. The bed frame had broken in the middle and fallen to the floor, causing our friend to snap like a pocket-knife. A cognac after the commotion and a replacement bed put his and our world back in order.

Cecilia developed a special love for my garden, which was overgrown. I didn't think it was that bad, but she wanted the garden to be neat and tidy. We agreed that she would design the garden according to her own ideas, but that she would leave a shady corner of the garden at the back, which had been almost untouched until then, untouched and left to nature - a little piece of German jungle!

Somehow, we survived the nasty legal dispute with Cecilia's ex-husband, even though she was left with an open wound - the sparse contact with her son Abdon. Even these few contacts were often cold and unsatisfactory; you could tell that Abdon was strongly influenced by his father against his mother. We enjoyed our relationship all the more, which quickly strengthened and soon formed a stable basis for a future together. We are very different in many ways, almost opposites, but have found that these opposites complement each other wonderfully to form a harmonious whole.

Due to our different preferences and abilities, we organized our household like a state. Cecilia was given the powerful "Ministry of the Interior", which meant she was responsible for the furnishings, among other things, something we would never have been able to agree on otherwise. She also got the "ministries" for family, food and agriculture (horticulture). I was left with the equally powerful "Ministry of Finance", as well as the departments of transport, construction and foreign relations (except the Far East) and the authority to issue directives, which was hardly ever used due to the successful distribution of tasks. Our "state" organized in this way functioned excellently, our partnership was harmonious and affectionate from the very beginning. I had arrived. While Ursula had been the secret love of my first half of life, with Cecilia I had finally found a new great love for the rest of my life.

New Ideas and Island Dreams

I didn't want to stay at the chemical plant for too long either. After some initial disputes with the works council, I had established myself quite well in the company. Among other things, I had gained a good reputation and respect by setting up a rescue service with an in-house ambulance. However, I soon realized that this job had no future for me. For one thing, the air in the chemical plant was always polluted with irritants, so my mild chronic bronchitis became more and more noticeable. On the other hand, contrary to my own convictions, I had to overlook some of the stresses and hazards caused by the substances and processes used, which I couldn't accept in the long term.

We had been toying with a completely different idea for some time. Our preferred destination at the time was Spain, the mainland, but above all the Canary Islands. We began to dream of settling on one of these islands and running a medical practice there together. This idea was made possible and supported by the newly adopted freedom of establishment within the European Union. The islands of Tenerife and La Palma were shortlisted for us. The ideas were already so concrete that I made an appointment with the mayor of the capital of La Palma, Santa Cruz de La Palma, and traveled to the island especially for a meeting. I asked him whether the population would accept a German doctor and he assured me that this would not be a problem. On the contrary, German doctors are held in high esteem in Spain. Alternatively, we negotiated with a large hotel in Puerto de la Cruz on Tenerife for suitable practice rooms. First of all, however, we had to obtain all the documents required to set up a practice in Spain and have them translated into Spanish - a bureaucratic challenge with the relevant authorities in both countries.

But then a family doctor was found dead in his practice in neighboring Ratingen.

They wanted to leave Düsseldorf and move to another country. I was to be sold in order to start a new life on an island. And this after I had just regained a new and quite respectable shape thanks to Cecilia's dedicated efforts! It wasn't just me who was horrified; my landlord´s family and friends were also less than enthusiastic about this plan. And so, the general relief was almost palpable when, shortly before the plan was to be implemented - five to twelve, so to speak - everything suddenly changed completely.

Running a Medical Practice

Suddenly everything had to happen very quickly. I was offered the opportunity to take over this GP practice. However, a binding decision was required within a few days. It seemed like a great, perhaps even unique opportunity to take over an existing and well-established practice close to my home without having to move. Within a few days, our island dreams were off the table, at least temporarily. But the idea wasn't completely dead yet. We accepted the offer and quit our previous jobs. This was rather naïve and gullible, as we were unable to really assess the value of this practice in the short term and had to rely on information from colleagues who were friends of the deceased's family. Ignorant as we were, we paid far too high a price for this practice. In fact, the purchase decision turned out to be a flop in the short term, but ultimately a stroke of luck for our lives in the long term.

The late colleague's practice was very run-down, and its equipment was completely outdated. A structural refurbishment and new equipment were unavoidable. Nevertheless, I had to pay the widow a not inconsiderable settlement for the existing patient base. Together with the necessary renovations, conversions and new equipment, the total sum amounted to over DM 300,000, despite many personal contributions. This was an advance payment without earning a single penny. The contract also provided for the employment of two medical assistants. What was initially an advantage, as they already knew the patients, later proved to be a disaster.

On April 1, 1988, after the renovations, alterations and purchases, we were able to open for business, and it was only then that the full extent of the catastrophically run-down practice became apparent. A good portion, around a third of the already rather small patient base of around 800 patients per quarter, had been thoroughly spoiled by my predecessor's problematic prescription policy. These patients had become accustomed to regular, medically unjustifiable prescriptions of addictive medication and unfounded certificates of incapacity for work. They now expected such prescriptions from me too. Of course, they could no longer get these prescriptions from me, which led to long discussions and sometimes even arguments, which put a lot of strain on Cecilia as the headnurse and on me. Many of these patients were persuaded, others left the practice disappointed, and the already small patient base became even smaller in the first year. The colleagues from the Association of Statutory Health Insurance Physicians who were friends with the widow must have been aware of the conditions in this practice. The purchase price they negotiated in no way did justice to these desolate conditions. We felt cheated.

However, word of the new tone and the new atmosphere in the practice spread around the town, so that new patients gradually registered and the situation in the practice slowly recovered. Cecilia contributed a lot to this new atmosphere. The warm tone at reception, her loving care of the patients, fresh flowers and the offer of fresh coffee in the tidy waiting room created a friendly and relaxed atmosphere. There were also special new treatments for certain cases, such as infusion therapies, which were gladly accepted by the patients.

But I didn't want to let my experience as a company doctor go to waste. So, I shortened my consultation hours on Thursday mornings and took on a job as a company doctor at a nearby IT company. This gave me a little extra income and a welcome break from the daily routine at the practice. Cecilia and the assistants took over the routine work in the practice during this time. To compensate for the reduced consultation hours, the afternoon consultation hours on Tuesdays and Thursdays were extended until 20:00. This was also intended as a service for working people. In reality, however, it was mostly pensioners who came to the practice during the additional evening hours. Another job as a company doctor was as a temporary replacement for the company doctor at Rheinbahn AG, which operates streetcars and buses in Düsseldorf. My main task there was to check the fitness to drive of the drivers with regular compulsory examinations, e.g. for indications of significant alcohol consumption. Such a finding then led to the driver being transferred to work as a control conductor, an extremely unpopular job. When I once managed to get a streetcar driving instructor back on duty by proving that his elevated liver enzymes were not due to alcohol, he fulfilled an old childhood dream for me out of gratitude. I was allowed to drive a streetcar through Düsseldorf under his supervision! Sweaty but happy, I brought the streetcar back to the depot after two hours.

The new management of the practice by Cecilia and me was not so well received by the two assistants who had taken over. They had clearly felt more at home in the old, sloppy environment. They were unreliable, rebellious and thieving when it came to little things like gifts from visitors or stamps. All in all, they were reluctant to work, but always ready to help themselves to the practice's property. We watched for a while, but at some point, it was enough. One Friday afternoon, the two of them were fired together without notice due to recent events. For us and our practice, however, that meant real distress for the time being. In the months that followed, we had to do all the work in the practice on our own. But we managed that too. We were then able to convince Cecilia's friend Annie, also a ward headnurse at Ratingen Catholic Hospital, to join us in making the practice a success. She took over the management of the practice so that Cecilia could concentrate on the medical services. With two experienced nurses, our practice was excellently staffed, which, after some initial irritation at the immediate dismissals, quickly got around the town. The reputation of the practice was further enhanced.

Nevertheless, I was not really satisfied with the results of the practice. There was plenty of work: consultation hours, home visits, a lot of bureaucracy with the health insurance companies and a 24-hour on-call service with occasional night shifts. A GP practice is anything but a 40-hour job. But the work was a lot of fun for the three of us and the feeling of being able to help was very satisfying. On the other hand, the income I earned was simply too low for this demanding medical work. It was nowhere near the level of my previous job as a company doctor. My two experienced headnurses caused high operating costs, and the turnover, i.e. the number of patients, could not be effectively increased in the small town with a second, well-established GP. There were hardly any private patients anyway. In addition, the premises were too small even for the existing patient base. A move to larger and more modern premises would have been necessary. In this situation, there was a fortunate coincidence of two events: I found an interested party who was prepared to take over the practice at short notice and, via my friend Peter, I received an attractive job offer from the pharmaceutical industry.

A Thursday Surprise

Despite the difficulties described above, we also enjoyed all the work in the practice. Neither of us would want to miss these experiences and memories. A warm relationship developed with many patients, and we also received a lot of recognition and respect for our work. A special experience during our time at the practice was our wedding on December 13, 1990, a Thursday.

It was a very strange marriage proposal that took place at the breakfast table in my kitchen sometime in October 1990. It wasn't the man who got down on one knee and asked the question of all questions. It was Cecilia, and she didn't get down on one knee either. Even the question was unusual. Between coffee and bread rolls, she didn't ask: "Will you marry me?" Instead, the question was: "When are we going to get married?" It didn't sound like a question either, but more like a demand. The answer wasn't a spontaneous, enthusiastic and tearful "yes" either, but rather a hesitant, thoughtful "well, if we're going to do it, we should do it this year". A couple had just got engaged here, both sides of whom were marked by divorce, including the "house finance minister", who already had his eye on the tax return for 1990.

And we made it. The registry office gave us an appointment on that Thursday at 11 a.m., before December 31. Thursday was also very convenient for me, as I didn't have office hours on Thursday mornings due to my company medical duties. But there wasn't enough time to prepare a big wedding celebration, everything had to happen quickly. So, the wedding ceremony took place in a very small circle. Only our best men, Annie and her husband Pags and my old friend Christoph, and my friend Rainer as photographer were there. We had chosen our favorite steakhouse for lunch afterwards.

The family celebration then took place shortly before Christmas at Georghausen Castle in the countryside near Cologne. But initially, after the wedding ceremony, there was just a card with the heading "Late Harvest" and the following text:

*"We had to build some bridges to find us;
we learnt to search our luck in profundity
and to let it grow in silence;
we silently married."*

This text in three languages, German, English and Spanish, took me a long evening and a bottle of red wine. The family was understandably a little dismayed to only find out about our decision by letter and afterwards. But in the end, everyone was delighted. Dad greeted our letter with a large cognac.

The card was also posted on the notice board of our practice on the day of our wedding before the consultation started at 2.00 pm. And it wasn't long before the first patient spotted the card and asked Cecilia incredulously if it was today. After that, everything happened very quickly. The news spread like wildfire in the small town. In any case, that same day, many gifts from dear patients arrived at the practice, where I also held my consultation that Thursday until 8 pm. There were flowers, wine, champagne, sweets, but also fresh fruit and vegetables. The flood of gifts continued over the next few days. Fortunately, I now had a larger car, a Nissan SUV, which I could use to drive the many gifts home. We were very pleased with the great interest my patients showed in our wedding. It was a wonderful recognition of our work.

They had both finally arrived! Neither of them was a blank slate, as they had experienced some turbulence in their previous lives. Then they had found each other, the doctor and the nurse, just like in the novel. A family catastrophe in Cecilia's first marriage had unexpectedly brought them together. Now, after a long period of mutual understanding and living together, they were both ready to shape the second and probably last phase of their lives together. Peace, harmony and order had long since returned into my walls. I could look to the future with confidence.

Assisted Traveling

Dad began to feel his age. At the age of 70, he was still physically and mentally very fit, with an almost unbridled desire to travel and with sufficient financial means, he still wanted to show his younger second wife

Gretel something of the world. But group trips were not his thing, and he no longer dared to set off alone as a couple into the wide, foreign-speaking world.

My relationship with Dad, which had often not been unclouded in my youth and during my studies, had improved considerably after completing my medical studies and especially after my marriage to Cecilia. In the meantime, it had become a very cordial relationship with mutual respect. It was only when it came to planning for his old age that Dad was less accessible. We had repeatedly tried to develop a longer-term plan for the future with him. In this context, we had also offered them both the opportunity to move into our house in Düsseldorf in due course, knowing full well that this would have involved considerable renovation and reconstruction work. They were delighted with this offer, but repeatedly turned it down. Their plan was simply to stay in their own home for as long as possible and then - let's see, no discussion.

To fulfill Dad's travel dreams, we planned our first big trip together to Mexico in 1991. All in all, this trip was a very nice experience and a great joy for the two old people. It could have been even better if Gretel hadn't insisted on taking her cousin Elfriede with her. Elfriede was a terrible "pain in the ass" who almost always had something to complain about and put my patience as a tour guide to the test.

The success of this first big trip together soon had us planning another trip - without Elfriede - and then another and another... The trips mostly went to the USA, to the west coast, to the big nature parks, to the east coast, to the Mississippi and to Florida. The longest trip took us to Chile, where Dad supported a sponsored child. From there we went on to Brazil to the Iguacu Falls and to Rio de Janeiro. Gretel's dream of one day standing on the Sugar Loaf Mountain came true on her birthday. The last trip in 2001 took them back to Washington and New York. But by then, the two old people's strength was already failing, so further long-distance trips were out of the question. Dad was already 82 years old at the time. He had significantly improved his English during these years of travel and gave a remarkable speech in English on my 50th birthday in 1998.

In the Pharmaceutical World

Sometimes coincidence also shapes the course of life. Peter was one of the most loyal pharmaceutical representatives in our practice and we had become friends with him and his wife Karin over the years. At some point, he moved from another company to Schwarz Pharma and often told me enthusiastically about the good working atmosphere there. He was also aware of my involvement in professional politics in the Association of Statutory Health Insurance Physicians and my interest in current politics. The pharmaceutical companies were also concerned about developments in healthcare policy at the time. One day in the office, Peter told me that Schwarz Pharma was planning to set up a staff unit for healthcare policy and asked me if I would be interested. I was, and he arranged an initial interview at the company, which was soon followed by an offer for the position.

Surprisingly quickly, and this was the second coincidence, I found a serious interested party to take over my practice: a senior consultant in internal medicine from a clinic in the Ruhr area wanted to set up his own business and bought the practice from me at a fair price. So, I was able to start my new job at Schwarz Pharma on March 1, 1993. It was unusual at first, a completely different life to the one I had in the practice. At 8.30 in the morning, I was no longer sitting in the darkened ultrasound booth looking into the inside of some tummies, but mostly in some conference room or on a plane to Berlin or other cities. I had many interesting conversations with opinion leaders or political decision-makers. Over the next 14 years, my position in the company evolved from health policy officer to Head of Corporate Communications. My duties also included a total of over 500 presentations, mostly to medical colleagues, on current health policy issues. Cecilia worked for my successor in the practice for another year and then found another job in a nearby care home for the elderly. Our fleet of vehicles also became more generous. Soon we had a pharmaceutical Mercedes at the door and Cecilia was able to replace her Polo with the previous family car, a large Citroën called "Sedan Chair".

The new situation was also very advantageous for me, the house. Running the practice together was very labor-intensive for both of them, often late into the evening, and brought a certain hectic pace to everyday life. There was simply little free time for other tasks. Now Cecilia and Annie were no longer co-entrepreneurs, but only employees of the new practice owner with regular working hours. The landlord now also had regular hours. He soon developed a knack for limiting business trips to one day if possible and being back home the same evening. This was not always possible, but very often. This left the young couple much more time to take care of other things, such as the maintenance and upkeep of their home. Repairs were carried out or commissioned and work was also done on the interior. Among other things, I got a new heating system and a new kitchen. That was good for me.

Party Time - in a Different Way

I was approaching 50 and I wanted to celebrate. But a party in the style of my 30s was of course out of the question. You get older, along with your circle of friends, which had also grown in the meantime. In the end, the final guest list included 72 people. So, we decided to hold the party in what was then "Düsseldorf's Living Room", the Heinrich Heine Hall in the Steigenberger Park Hotel at the beginning of the famous Königsallee. Especially for our Filipino guests, the family of Cecilia's sister Nelia, we moved the celebration from the cold

German February to May 2, 1998. I appointed myself program director and host. Between the individual courses of the big dinner, there was a varied program of scenes, speeches, pictures, games and music. Many friends took part in the program with their own contributions, and Dad also tried his hand at a witty English speech. Other highlights included a performance by a dance sports group, a Filipino light dance and a rousing belly dance by Angela, Cecilia's godchild. The absolute highlight came after dessert: a drummer brought over 50 different rhythm instruments into the hall, from which everyone was allowed to choose one. These instruments were then used to rehearse an African song together. It worked surprisingly well, so that in the end we all put on a remarkable musical performance together. However, this had to be abruptly interrupted when the receptionist stormed in at around 1 a.m. and urgently asked us to stop making noise, as some hotel guests had already complained to him. There couldn't have been a better way to end the party!

Although the actual party didn't take place here ~ and that was a good thing, because I'm getting older too ~ it was a turbulent weekend for me too. Some guests spent the night here, the breakfast buffets were huge, and the bathroom was always full. But they were happy days, and everyone felt at home here. Over the next few days, I found many thank~you letters in my letterbox.

There was also Donnie, the younger son of Nelia and Dante. His real name is Marc Danielle. We had a lot of fun when he helped me with the preparations for the party. After work, he got his very first beer at Pilsner Urquell in the Old City at the age of 17. He really enjoyed it and it made him quite funny. Unfortunately, Donnie was to make tragic news a little later...

A Fatal Bus Ride

On July 16, 2000, Donnie was murdered on a public bus in Manila. He was on his way home from high school. Several men forced their way onto the bus and shot him in the head. There was no apparent motive, Donnie was probably just in the wrong place at the wrong time. The perpetrators initially managed to escape but were later caught and convicted by the police.

For the shocked family of Nelia, Dante and Donnie's siblings Eric and Jennifer, it was sheer horror, a catastrophe. They were devastated and needed support, and we wanted to give it to them. The very next day, I was able to organize a flight to Manila for Cecilia to accompany the family to the funeral. She then obtained the necessary visas for visits to Germany from the German embassy in Manila. Just two weeks after her return, Jennifer, Donnie's younger sister, came to stay with us for six months on an extended visa. In September, Nelia followed for three months and in December Dante joined her for the remaining time. Despite all the grief, the family didn't let it get them down - and Cecilia, the older sister, played a major part in this.

Family Crisis Management

Jennifer was the most difficult. Shocked, in mourning, with a still very childlike disposition and depressive mood swings, she went through a difficult time. In order to come to terms with what had happened, it was necessary for her to get out of the environment of the horrific crime. After a settling-in period, she felt very comfortable in her new surroundings with us and was now ready for a fresh start. The only thing she didn't like was sleeping alone and in the dark. So, she moved into the small room next to our bedroom, separated from ours only by a curtain, and kept a small bedside lamp on all night. We entertained her, kept her distracted and occupied and cheered her up a little with activities and programs. Cecilia took her with her to work in the nursing home and quickly realized that she enjoyed working with the elderly. But the lively young woman was also an enrichment for them, and the old people really enjoyed her.

When Nelia, Cecilia's sister, arrived from the Philippines, the mood became melancholier again. She, too, had to bear the brunt of her son's brutal death. There were long conversations in our living room, with Cecilia skillfully taking on the role of an empathetic moderator who kept steering Nelia's thoughts away from the past and towards a positive future.

As if that wasn't enough of a problem, one evening Abdon, now 20 years old and a new student of business informatics, turned up at the door with his first girlfriend Marie. After a heated argument with his father, he had thrown him out of the apartment. Abdon hadn't shown his face for a long time, he must have thought we were pretty bad people after his father's constant reproaches. But now he was here and asked for help in his time of need. His girlfriend Marie couldn't or wouldn't take him in either - a young couple who had literally had the rug pulled out from under them. In the meantime, Nelia had moved in upstairs with Jennifer next to our bedroom, so we were able to offer Abdon our guest room for the time being and let him stay there. But of course, this could only be a temporary solution; after a few weeks Abdon found a small apartment of his own in Ratingen. He continued to receive financial support from his father. For us, and especially for Cecilia, the expulsion was a stroke of luck, because Abdon found his way back to us. A new, wonderful parental relationship began with a detailed discussion between mother and son. There were tears, insight and a reconciliatory new beginning.

The quiet existence of a working couple in a large house was over. It became full again, lots of life within my walls, lots of grief and lots of conversations, lots of problems and solutions, but all in a beautiful community. The kitchen was - very Filipino - the central meeting place. My living room, which is otherwise rarely used, also became the center of many long conversations. The biggest family crisis meeting was when Abdon and Marie arrived unexpectedly. The causes and solutions to the problem were discussed around the living room table.

In the midst of this Philippine turmoil, I was given a week off. Even before these dramatic events, I had signed up for a one-week Spanish course in Antigua/Guatemala and booked the flights and accommodation. As living together in the house worked well and most conversations were held in Tagalog, the local Filipino language, there was no good reason for me to cancel the planned trip. So, I flew with Lufthansa via Mexico City to Guatemala City and from there by bus to Antigua, where I found a sparsely furnished but spacious room in my accommodation, an old villa. The lessons essentially consisted of an eight-hour conversation per day with my teacher, including a one-hour lunch break, which I also needed. We told each other stories from our lives, and whenever necessary, she helped me with new words or grammatical corrections. The course was exhausting, but also relaxing due to the total change of environment and topics. In the beautiful small town of Antigua, you quickly get used to the regular small earthquakes caused by the surrounding volcanoes. And so, back at home, I brought a new and healthy dose of serenity for the agitated situation there.

After a lovely Christmas with the whole family, the host family's stability was restored to such an extent that they were able to return to the Philippines. The house was ours again.

What influence do you think I had on stabilizing the shocked family? I don't think my influence should be underestimated. The tranquil surroundings of my location provided the necessary contrast to the hustle and bustle of the megacity of Manila, where the drama had unfolded. My sturdy walls convey safety and security. The cozy interior with its warm colors creates a calming environment and the setting for long, undisturbed conversations. These were very good conditions for coping with the great shared grief. In the much more turbulent living environment in the Philippines, the grieving process would certainly have been much more difficult. But I'm just giving the background; Cecilia undoubtedly did most of the coping.

Conquering the World

Normality returned to the old walls. We both went about our jobs, which had long since stabilized and settled down. Our everyday lives were regular and unspectacular. Leisure time, visits to and from friends, joint and individual activities were also enjoyable. What was new was that my new job had given me a financial stability that had previously been rather alien to me. Even when I had my own practice, finances had always been a critical issue. The overdraft on the current account was a more or less constant companion. The new stability allowed us to pursue a shared hobby, traveling, more than before. I myself had always traveled a lot, preferably to South America, even when money was tight. However, these trips were always dictated by the cheapest flights and extremely tight travel budgets. However, they were no less beautiful and eventful because of the many impressions and experiences from other countries. I was often smiled at incredulously in South America when I told people that I was traveling with very little money in my pocket. It didn't fit into the world view of the people living there that a European would undertake such trips without a major financial background. Nobody there believed my story of the "poor student".

Now we were able to travel together on a decent level as part of our annual vacation, and we made the most of this opportunity. Our favorites in those years were Spain and Italy, but also other European countries. There were also many long-distance trips, especially to the USA, South America, the Caribbean, South Africa and the Philippines. We mostly preferred shorter trips, but there were more of them. Our desire to travel grew almost unchecked and was to continue in the years that followed.

Cecilia's Birthday

In 2004, Cecilia's 60th birthday was just around the corner. In the meantime, working conditions in the nursing home had deteriorated more and more. There was a constant shortage of staff, which was partly compensated for by less competent assistants from abroad. This was hardly successful, so Cecilia had to do more and more work in addition to her duties to at least partially compensate for the gaps and omissions of other employees in caring for the patients. I was worried that she would suffer health problems due to the constant physical overload. We therefore decided together that she should apply for early retirement at the age of 60 with the appropriate deductions. And that's what happened. After a long time, the house was now home to a pensioner again.

In addition to the pension issue, I also realized that you can't just go back to business as usual when you turn 60. Until then, we had been in the habit of traveling on our birthdays and celebrating these occasions together. But that was out of the question for her 60th. A party was needed, and not just any party, but the big one. A suitable location was quickly found: Rheinfels Castle near Sankt Goar, one of the largest and most beautiful historic castles in the Rhineland with a good hotel and restaurant. The manager of the hotel was very helpful with the planning and preparations. Under strict secrecy, I teamed up with Abdon to prepare the program. The program included a historical balladeer for the reception, a magic show by the head of the house himself, a festive menu, a speech by me, a singing performance by Abdon, a belly dance by Angela, Cecilia's godchild, and a speech by Dad. There were also a few speeches and songs from our guests. The highlight of the program was a firework display in the castle courtyard at midnight, during which the name "Cecilia" was painted in glowing letters on the castle wall. This had been organized for us by the head of the castle. The local fire department was also dutifully present during the fireworks display and was kept in good spirits beforehand with a hearty meal and beer in the cellar bar. It was a big party, just as we had hoped, with a good 70 guests, including guests from Norway, Switzerland and the Philippines. Our Norwegian friends Jostein and Randi stayed with us for a few days. It was a special experience for Jostein to drive from our house to the castle and back with Nelia and Dante in a large, borrowed Mercedes. And last but not least, Cecilia's sensational breakfast buffets will live long in the memory.

An Unlikely Team on a Visit

During a visit to Peru with Cecilia, Teresa asked us if we could also make it possible for her daughter Melissa to visit Germany. It was an expensive but also wonderful idea for us to give the young woman this opportunity. So, we planned and prepared for Melissa to visit us in the summer of 2007. She was almost 20 years old at the time and was preparing for her medical studies. Melissa then stayed with us for three weeks.

At the same time, Sarah, the then nine-year-old daughter of our friends Hartmut and Sakura from northern Germany, insisted on being allowed to visit us alone at home. This was also a wish of both of us. As a result, we had a young girl and a young woman staying with us at the same time for a week. A team that could hardly be more different!

Melissa was rather different from her mother Teresa. Teresa was always attentive, nimble and was always ready to help wherever she could. Her daughter, on the other hand, was more calm and not so active. Even her arrival at Amsterdam Airport was - through no fault of her own - chaotic. Her flight was delayed and the last connecting flight of the day had already departed. Her suitcase could not be found and had disappeared. We went by car to Amsterdam late in the evening and picked her up there. During the first days of her stay we were mainly busy with lifting her up from that shock and getting her dressed and kitted out. Melissa felt comfortable with us but did not spontaneous participate in the household - our dear Peruvian princess. Obviously not knowing of the German virtue of punctuality, Melissa did not take appointments for getting up and breakfast too seriously, what gave us sometimes problems with planning our tours with her or meetings with friends. But all in all, Melissa seemed to like our program and so we hoped that she had something positive to tell her mother. Unfortunately, her luggage including her new suitcase and new outfits was again stolen on her return flight!

Sarah, on the other hand, at nine years old and about ten years younger than Melissa, was lively, bubbly and loud, but always attentive and helpful. She was really looking forward to the visit and showed it. Sometimes she was a bit of a handful because she constantly wanted to be entertained and kept busy. Sarah had a vivid imagination and loved role-playing games. Her favorite game was Titanic, where she played the ship, I played the waves and Cecilia played the string orchestra. Melissa tended to play the iceberg. And so, we would sit on the terrace in the evening and let the Titanic sink again and again while the string orchestra played on tirelessly and the waves never let up.

After completing her medical degree, Melissa can already look back on a successful career as a doctor. Sarah is now studying International Relations at the University of Münster and at various universities abroad.

Dad Leaves

Dad was now clearly showing his age. Health problems kept him in hospital for several days at a time. And they also meant that his hitherto remarkable mental freshness was now fading. Our two old people in Brühl-Vochem increasingly became our problem children. Dad was often visited by young, eloquent representatives who obviously knew exactly where old people lived. He would then gullibly sign dubious contracts from time to time, for example for unnecessary and expensive renovation work on his house. Gerd always put things right afterwards by getting the agents to cancel the contracts. Dad also occasionally got lost in the city, where he was soon no longer a stranger. The police or a friendly bus driver usually brought him home again. Often, the bus even stopped in front of our house to bring him home safely.

Overall, the lion's share of the increasingly necessary care for the two elderly people was left to Gerd, who devoted a lot of time to this task alongside his other voluntary work. We also often visited the two old people in Brühl, usually on Sundays, to take them out for lunch at Dad's beloved steakhouse. But he was increasingly dependent on help with his meals. The waiters already knew him and were aware of this. Without being asked, there was always a large pile of napkins on the table. Dad's house suffered increasingly from a lack of care. Necessary renovations were repeatedly postponed. The cleanliness also left a lot to be desired. Even with dedicated help, it became more and more clear that things could not go on like this. A move to assisted living became unavoidable. However, we all had to do a lot of persuading, as the two elderly people kept rejecting the idea. Finally, one day Cecilia made the breakthrough. The move was accepted, and Gerd immediately set to work. He found a beautiful new retirement home with a care unit near his house. However, in the last few weeks before the move at the beginning of 2008, Dad's health deteriorated dramatically, and he was admitted directly to the nursing home. He died there a few days later. So, Gretel lived alone in the beautiful two-room apartment that Gerd had chosen for them both. She died a year later, in 2009, and they both found their final resting place in the family grave at the cemetery in Vochem.

What was to happen to Dad's house, which was just over 30 years old? It was not in good condition; renovations were urgently needed and much of the furniture was worn or unsightly. The house's biggest drawback, however, was its remote location on the outskirts of the village, right next to a nature reserve and far from any good transport links. This location, which is very popular with burglars, had led to several break-ins in the house. For this reason alone, there was no serious interested party in the extended family circle. The sale was correspondingly difficult, and the price achieved was rather unsatisfactory.

But that wasn't the worst of it: the sale was preceded by clearing out and decluttering. It was a Herculean task! None of us had any idea how much stuff there could be in a house that wasn't that big. It was simply overwhelming, with one container after another filling up. I didn't count them, but there were a lot. In retrospect, Dad turned out to be a real collector. In addition to his study and company documents, the cupboards also contained all the plans for his many trips - including flight tickets and hotel brochures. And last but not least, all the preparatory materials for his famous theme evenings. The extensive library proved to be largely worthless and eventually filled a large paper container after no buyer could be found. Old and ancient clothing had to be searched through, as many pockets still contained banknotes and coins. After all, this effort was worth it, as a considerable amount was collected. The "clear ship" campaign for the house took weeks - and there was still a lot for the buyer to do.

At this point, I have to speak up again: I, too, am feeling a not inconsiderable sense of fullness. I'm afraid that I'll have to do a similar clean-up and clear-out at some point. And it could turn out to be much bigger than Dad's when I look at my rooms and everything that's there. Perhaps my residents would be well advised to take precautions in this respect and gradually dispose of their unnecessary stuff now. But as if you're talking to walls...

New Independence

My employment with Schwarz Pharma ended on March 31, 2008. Not entirely voluntarily, the reason was the sale of the company to the Belgian pharmaceutical group UCB. One of the attractions of such a merger for the entrepreneur is the potential savings. Similar functions in both companies, which would then be duplicated, can be reduced to one department. This was also the case in my area of work. There was a colleague at UCB who had similar tasks to mine at Schwarz Pharma. Instead of competing to see which of us could stay, we sat down together and found a better joint solution. My offer to my colleague was to voluntarily give up my position in the company. In return, she agreed to provide me with orders from our field of activity as an external agency. We quickly came to an agreement, which the company then honored with a fair severance payment for me. In the years that followed, the cooperation we had agreed upon was excellent and in a good atmosphere; we became friends. This solution was by no means inconvenient for me. I had reached the age of 60 and was already thinking about continuing my work on an independent basis. This plan was made easier by the fact that I had already also been working on a freelance basis for several years with the company's permission. These were, for example, lectures at training events for doctors or editorial tasks. So, I didn't have to start my new self-employment from scratch but could fall back on sufficient start-up capital and an existing client list.

And again, a valuable friendship also benefited me professionally. During my time at Schwarz Pharma, I had established business contacts with an editorial office for health policy in Berlin and met the editor-in-chief Thomas there in 2006. We soon met up with him and his Korean wife HeuiSuk in private and became good friends. A first highlight of this friendship was my pilgrimage with Thomas on the Way of St. James in 2007. We subsequently wrote a small book together about the impressions and experiences of this journey. Many more trips together with the wives were to follow - to Europe, the USA and even the Philippines. But incidentally, this friendly connection to health policy events in Berlin was also invaluable for my new professional ambitions. Thomas made my new start in self-employment much easier. With the founding of a limited company for these activities, my final career change from pharmaceutical manager to journalist was sealed.

The new job also had a big impact on our everyday life at home. I no longer had to drive to Monheim every morning to get home more or less on time in the evening. The day now usually started with a leisurely breakfast together and then reading the newspaper. After that, I usually retired to my study to complete the tasks at hand. There were still the frequent, usually roughly weekly business trips to Berlin. However, I was almost always able to limit these to one or at most two days. Cheap flights between the two cities made this possible. In addition to my journalistic work, I took on a teaching position at the Charité hospital in Berlin. I really enjoyed working with the students. I later described my impressions from this work and my experiences with the students in my first book "Becoming a doctor". Even though this book was not a great sales success, it was always very welcome as a small gift to friends and customers.

The House Enjoys a New Shine

I also benefited greatly from my residents' career changes. Both were now at home most of the time and had much more time to think about and initiate repairs and changes. For me, it was like a rejuvenating cure. The biggest thing that was done in 2009 was the renovation of the floors on the first and second floors and the stairs. The carpeting in the upstairs living room was ripped out, including all the layers that were still between it and the original wooden floor. A pedestal in the office, on which the desk with armchair and some shelves stood, was also dismantled and removed. The pedestal had once been installed so that the master of the house could look out of the window while working. All the furniture on the upper floors was then cleared out or at least moved. The landlord hired three students for this sometimes-difficult work, who worked with great enthusiasm and skill and completed the work much faster than originally planned. Accordingly, they were happy that the planned budget allowed for a higher hourly wage. Then three professionals arrived with heavy equipment to sand down my old wooden floorboards and remove the ugly reddish-brown paint ("bull's blood"). In the end, everyone was delighted with the result, which could only be guessed at beforehand. It was fresh, light-colored wood that was sealed with clear varnish. This gave my staircase in particular a friendlier look. The light-colored wood of the staircase made everything appear in a new light. The rooms on the first floor, the stairs to the attic and the entire attic floor also benefited. Everything looked like new! A week of deafening noise and lots of dust from the sanding was torture for the residents and the whole neighborhood. But for me ~ the house ~ it was definitely worth it!

A Break-In with Expensive Consequences

We were burgled. The thieves came through the garden at lunchtime, shortly after we had left the house for a visit to the city. The old and somewhat dilapidated fence was little match for them. They didn't even bother to pry open the patio door, which wouldn't have been too difficult. It was probably quicker to smash a hidden side window with a stone and enlarge the entrance hole with a flowerpot. They worked carefully and without causing any other major damage or devastation. However, they were unable to complete their work as we returned home unexpectedly early. An accomplice must have warned them by cell phone. They left the house the same way they had entered. They had searched the cellar, the ground floor and the bedroom in the attic. Fortunately, the first floor remained untouched - and therefore the only rooms in which they could have found money and jewelry. Our burglars must have been particularly disappointed in the cellar. Our safe had already been broken into and was empty, as Cecilia had accidentally broken the key in the lock shortly beforehand. Despite our annoyance, we enjoyed a moment of schadenfreude together with the police who had arrived.

Before the break-in, we had already replaced the front door and the cellar door with new, very sturdy metal doors. "You don't even try to break in through these doors," said the salesman. Then you just try another way. And indeed, the 40-year-old and barely secured windows were now the house's major weak point. After the break-in, the first thing we did was to replace the dilapidated garden fence with a sturdy, two-meter-high metal fence. Although this is not insurmountable, it is at least a first significant hurdle.

Then it was on to the windows. We knew it would be expensive. The house has 19 windows in very different sizes, from the tiny window in the guest toilet to the terrace front with double doors and side windows. The windows had to have sturdy glazing, all-round locking and lockable handles to make them highly resistant to attempted break-ins. A company that sells resistant windows was quickly found on the Internet. A window of resistance class 2 is on display in the store, where clients as "burglars" can try their hand at it with a hammer and screwdriver - and fail. This convinced us and we decided on this type of window. Very good sound and thermal insulation were other welcome features of the windows. Finally, an alarm system was installed. In total, we invested around 80,000 euros to secure our house and prevent any further break-ins.

The Emotional Transition to Retirement

The inevitable was getting closer and closer - and finally it arrived: the start of retirement age, three months after my 65th birthday. The relevant forms and correspondence were already filling up a large folder. And then they arrived, the pension notices from the various insurance providers - and finally, the pensioner's ID card. With a shudder, I took this piece of plastic out of the envelope and immediately into a drawer at the back. It has remained there untouched until now. I didn't really want to accept this new phase of my life yet. The new additional money in my account was much more welcome. That was helpful for me to accept the new situation and come to terms with it.

It was certainly also a fortunate circumstance that my work simply continued as if nothing had happened. My customers knew nothing about my new status. They simply wanted to continue receiving the agreed services. And so, I was able to carry on as before, pulling my press card out of my wallet when the opportunity arose instead of my unloved pensioner's ID card. "I can do this for another three years," I thought to myself, "or maybe until my 70th birthday at the most." I no longer advertised my work anyway. The existing customers turned out to be quite loyal. When the first customers dropped out at the age of 71, I saw this as a welcome opportunity to further reduce the amount of work. But I still did not really want to stop. Isn't this kind of development ideal? A slow winding down of professional activity without hard cuts and transitions? In any case, that is how we felt. We enjoyed having more time for ourselves, for example for a longer breakfast, a regular lunch break together and free time in the evening too. In between, we each had our own work so that we did not disturb each other. We spent most of the money that came in from my remaining job on travel. Traveling - sometimes together with Thomas and

HeuiSuk - became a regular and much-loved leisure activity in our retirement.

My story can also be watched to some extent in the cars that have been parked outside my front door over the years. All in all, a pretty impressive fleet of vehicles came together. First there was the small Ford 12m, Dad's first car, followed later by larger models of the same make. Then came the small Citroen ("duck"), my Aachen engineering student's first car, and later a second "duck" from Gerd. After a Renault R4 and a small Peugeot 205 came the legendary VW buggy, which you could only start from the bottom, then a good, but also very old VW Beetle convertible. Just in time for medical school, the often-mentioned lime green BMW 1502 arrived on the doorstep, followed by a slightly larger white model of the same brand. The Chevrolet Monte Carlo, which my clinic doctor drove to work, took up most of the space outside the front door. The Peruvian "Princess" Maria was then displeased by a Peugeot 205GTI, which was far from the limousine she expected. My family doctor bought the first new car in this series, a Nissan Terrano SUV. In my pharmaceutical manager's time, several, mostly larger Mercedes models dominated, some of which were provided by his generous employer. In addition to his "sedan chair", a Citroën C5, my freelance journalist had a small Mercedes 200SLK coupé. Cecilia contributed a VW Golf and a VW Polo before she finally gave up driving altogether, exasperated. My pensioners made do with a modest Mercedes 200GLA for their increasingly infrequent trips.

Shortly after I retired, I received the sad news that my first love Ursula had died. We had still written to each other from time to time. After my last letter went unanswered, a short time later I received a text message from her husband with the news of the fatal outcome of her new cancer. As I also learned that Ursula wanted stones, especially Rhine pebbles, for her grave, I planned to get them and bring them to the grave. At that time, Nelia and Dante from the Philippines were visiting us. So, I took Dante to a stonemason to buy a large Rhine pebble. Dante was shocked when he found out the reason for the stone purchase. For days, he expressed his incomprehension about my plan to visit my old friend's grave. The visit went ahead anyway.

But there were also other nice events: I celebrated my 70th birthday in 2018 not at home, but with 65 guests on the top floor of a 16-storey hotel at Düsseldorf harbor. It was a cosy celebration with many dear friends without a big program. Our guests from Norway, France and Hamburg stayed for a few days. They stayed in the house and in a neighboring hotel so that we could be together for breakfast and in the evening on our terrace. In contrast, we spent Cecilia's 75th birthday in 2019 very privately in Sardinia on the Costa Smeralda. And finally, Teresa from Peru joined us again for ten days in 2019 after visiting a congress in Athens.

We were simply satisfied - with our daily routine, with our surroundings in the beautiful house, with many good friends and acquaintances and, of course, and especially with our health, which has been quite good so far. It could hardly have been better or more beautiful.

Reflections on the Future

The house probably still has a long life ahead of it. At least at the moment, it is not foreseeable that the development plans in this estate will change significantly. Despite the many sources of noise in the surrounding area - airplanes, freeway, main road and streetcar - this estate will probably remain an attractive residential area close to the city in the future.

For us, however, it is time to plan the final stage of our lives. Of course, it would be nice to stay in this house in familiar surroundings until the end of our lives. On the other hand, we know from our professional and family experience about the problems that would be associated with this. As good as our current state of health is, we know that this could change at short notice. And then we would be dependent on help and support at home. We don't see family help as a reality. We live alone and there is probably no capacity for this within reach. On the other hand, the prospect of permanent support from strangers in our own home fills us with concern. The risk of being poorly cared for or even deceived if we become increasingly helpless seems great to us. Relatives or friends who could keep an eye on the situation are too far away for such a permanent task.

The alternative would be to leave the house. In recent years, a number of new care options have been developed for senior citizens, e.g. senior-friendly apartments or shared apartments. However, such structures only solve part of the potential problems, as it is possible that people will need to move to a care facility later. The concept of a retirement home seems more convincing to us. This is an apartment in a house that offers all the necessary assistance up to and including full nursing care as an option. This solution, which is probably the most expensive, would give us the security of being equipped for all eventualities of necessary care. Ideally, we would only need the apartment in the long term and could do without the other services and options.

We thought that the decision to move into a retirement home should be made early on. Then you would still have enough flexibility to settle into the new environment and make new friends. But not too early either, on the other hand, as it is best to live in your own home and the residence is also a very expensive option. Finally, the average age of the residents in the residence is worth considering - who would want to be the youngest resident in such a residential complex? It's a difficult decision, not least because saying goodbye to your own four walls is associated with great emotion. Equally difficult is the question of whether we could even afford a nice apartment in a retirement home. Rental costs are likely to rise much faster than pension income, and then there may also be the cost of additional services. How long will the money last to bridge this difference? The question of how long it will finally last cannot be answered in advance anyway.

We have found a retirement home that we like and that also seems affordable. We recently signed a qualifying contract there. The contract does not oblige us to move in, but we will receive non-binding offers for available apartments of a suitable size. The first step has thus been taken and a viable path to the final stage of our lives has been mapped out.

A Pandemic Creates New Facts

A new, deadly coronavirus was first discovered in China at the end of 2019 and spread rapidly around the world. Many of those infected died in agony from pneumonia with severe respiratory distress. The intense global travel activity of our time has enabled the virus to spread so quickly and worldwide. It may have originated in China, but no one knows for sure; there are various speculations about its origins. In 2019, we were also still traveling carefree, in Ecuador and Peru with Abdon, in France on the Atlantic coast, in Singapore and Australia, in Vienna and in Martinique. Teresa also came to us from Peru in 2019. At the beginning of 2020, the extent of the threat was still underestimated, and we traveled to the Philippines with our friends Annedore and Jürgen without a care in the world. As soon as we returned to Germany, the pandemic development of the disease was also recognized here, and drastic measures were ordered.

A lockdown of public life and the obligation to wear a face mask now determined everyday life. Only the bare essentials could still be bought, and most stores remained closed. Hoarding purchases meant that even toilet paper became scarce. Office work was shifted as far as possible to the home, a new and not always pleasant experience for many families. Schools, kindergartens and universities were also closed, which placed an additional burden on families. The country was not equipped for the switch to online teaching; there was a lack of equipment, teaching programs and probably not enough flexible teachers. Everyone was asked to stay at home if possible and avoid contact with others. We felt quite privileged in this situation, as we were able to cope with the restrictions in our large house and garden. But the news about the many infections and deaths and about strict visiting bans, especially in retirement homes, made us very thoughtful about plans for our future.

Compared to our neighboring countries, the first wave of infections with the new virus in Germany was rather mild. But after a short break came the second, then the third and fourth waves with ever new restrictions in everyday life. Even the development and production of vaccines in a sensationally short time could not really stop the pandemic. Despite large-scale vaccination campaigns, it continued to rage until 2022 with several new virus variants. Today, the COVID-19 disease caused by the virus is no longer considered a pandemic, but it is still around, and quite common. Experts assume that COVID19, like the flu, will remain with us permanently. There were always calmer weeks or months between waves, which even allowed us to travel again. But the doubts about our plans remained.

A Disenchanting Analysis of the Situation

The mood in Germany has also deteriorated dramatically. Resentment at the measures and restrictions imposed because of the pandemic manifested itself in daily and increasingly aggressive demonstrations. Hatred and a willingness to violence increased in daily life and on social media. Stubborn refusal to vaccinate and conspiracy theories fueled each other and prevented full vaccination protection against the virus. Radical political currents, including the outright rejection of democracy, law and the state, are gaining ground. A general increase in selfishness is causing minorities to demand privileges for their particular interests. The failings of both the last and the current coalition government are becoming increasingly obvious. The transport infrastructure is falling into disrepair, digitalization is making no real progress and bureaucracy continues to flourish. The current governing coalition, the so-called "traffic light" government, started with big promises that are proving to be unrealistic in many important respects. The traffic light coalition is now deeply divided and there is no improvement in sight. Even the promised climate protection targets are likely to be missed by a wide margin. How could this be achieved in this ongoing dispute? The country is not in a good state at the moment.

Added to this are current external problems. Following a military attack by Russia, the long-simmering conflict between Russia and Ukraine has turned into a full-blown war that has now been going on for over two years. A diplomatic solution is a long way off. Neither side is prepared to enter into reasonable negotiations on the disputed issues. Although Europe condemns the military attack and supports the attacked Ukraine, it does not want to intervene itself in order to avoid an escalation. Moreover, there is no agreement in Europe on a joint approach even on this pressing issue. At the same time, Israel also started a war in the Gaza Strip following serious terrorist attacks by the Palestinian Hamas. The USA is divided due to constant domestic political disputes and is in permanent crisis mode, but at the same time is ready to assert its own interests militarily at any time. Now that Russia has largely stopped or had to stop supplying gas to Germany and most European countries, scarce gas supplies are causing energy prices to rise significantly, which has contributed to inflation in Germany and Europe. Even the rapid construction of liquefied natural gas terminals has hardly been able to fully replace Russian gas. Cold winters could lead to shortages of heating energy and even brownouts in the coming years. By then at the latest, public discontent is likely to reach a critical level.

Have we really learned nothing from two world wars? Or is it because those in power today have not personally experienced the horrors of war and have therefore forgotten them? Are the war experiences described here starting all over again? This is currently a bitter reality in Ukraine and the Gaza Strip.

Another "pandemic" seems to be upcoming, and that is the apparent increase in selfishness worldwide. Hatred and a willingness to use violence in society are just as much a consequence of this "disease" as armed conflicts in global politics. If citizens, officials, politicians, state leaders and nations only regard themselves and their own interests, then values and the basis of coexistence are lost, and conflicts are inevitable. This pandemic could become even more dangerous than COVID-19.

Doubts and Alternative Plans

The analysis of the current situation in the country is therefore quite disenchanting and creates worry lines on the forehead rather than anticipation for the near future. And once again, an external impulse has led our thoughts in a completely new direction. This time the impetus came from the Philippines. A few years ago, we already had the idea of setting up a senior citizens' shared appartment in the Philippines together with Nelia and Dante. At that time, however, the two of them were still too busy with their many tasks, so the idea soon disappeared into a drawer again.

The plan has now been resurrected due to recent events. On their last trip in December 2021, Cecilia, Nelia and Dante visited their brother Israel in Bataan, a beautiful area opposite Manila on Manila Bay. Israel has an influential position and good connections there. He would also be able to find us a nice house or a good plot of land there. The Bataan district has a good infrastructure. and the area is considered quiet and peaceful. And Nelia and Dante also see the idea with completely different eyes today than they did back then, namely very positively now. Dante has a small construction company, and this could be his last and biggest building project: A large, senior-friendly bungalow for the four of us.

But of course, this plan also raises questions. Leave your own country? For good? That would certainly not be an easy decision! It is still a plan B, the retirement home is not yet out of the question. Could it become plan A? However, there are still a few things to consider before making such a decision.

Financially, it might be the big one. Building or buying a house in the Philippines is much cheaper than here. And with a normal German pension, you can live very well there, the cost of living is lower. However, the political situation would not really improve. What do you hear about the Philippines? Some government decisions there seem arbitrary and often very strict. The police are omnipresent and take harsh and often brutal action. There is no rule of law as we understand it in Germany. The infrastructure is being developed but is still patchy. And finally, Taiwan is a critical trouble spot with the threat of war on the doorstep. Supplying the house and property, on the other hand, would not be a problem. A lot of help and support could be expected from the family, and external help is easier and much cheaper to get there than here. Any care that might be needed in old age would also be easy to organize and probably even better than the often-stressed care workers here.

Cecilia would find the move easier than me. She is happy in the Philippines, gets on very well with her large family and can also express herself and make herself understood much better in her own language there. In short, she feels at least as much at home there as she does here. Her main problem would be the great distance to Abdon and his family with the three grandchildren. And of course, also to my family and our dear mutual friends. Those are my problems too, but the dimension is much bigger for me. Professional and private contacts that have developed over decades are often still active, at least occasionally. Then there is the whole cultural German background, the language, the customs and traditions, the opportunities for education and entertainment, discussion and the exchange of experiences. Although today's means of communication make it easier to exchange ideas over long distances, they can only replace proximity to a limited extent. It would therefore be essential for me to spend several weeks in Europe at least twice a year in order to maintain existing bridges and recharge my cultural batteries. As long as I am physically able to do so.

Everything was still open, but we were in an intensive phase of research and planning for plan B, while plan A was still up in the air. In both cases, however, it was clear that the house was for sale. I put a lot of work, a lot of money, but also a lot of love into this house. At least the same goes for Cecilia in terms of work and love. In return, the house has given us safety, joy and a wonderful time within its walls. Our paths will now part. A new era will soon begin for Cecilia and me, as well as for the house.

What Will Happen to the House?

Yes, and what will become of me? Three generations of a family have made me what I am today. I was built in difficult circumstances, have lived through bad times, defied the bombs of the Second World War and harbored great hardship within my walls. Death came into my walls, but so did new life. Marriages were made, but also a divorce. And there were very good times here, too; there was a lot of love, laughter and celebrations. Life happened within my walls, just as it is. There was despair and suffering as well as love, happiness and joy. In my memory, harmony outweighs all the problems that have arisen. And just now, when the end of this era is looming, I too have found an inner beauty and satisfaction as an old house.

But what happens next? At the moment, everything points to me being sold. Cecilia's son Abdon has a family of his own and a house with a garden in a rural area near Düsseldorf. They show little inclination to move here, even though I am "naturally" bigger and nicer than the other house, at least from my point of view. I think the aircraft noise also plays a major role here. Even my landlord says that if the aircraft noise really bothers you, you shouldn't move here. Another point is that the landlord would need the money from the sale for his plans with the retirement home as well as for his plan B. So, most likely, the property will be sold.

Who should buy me? Here, in the immediate vicinity of the Düsseldorf trade fair and the airport, a company would probably pay the highest price for a house in this location. But would that suit me? Should a house with such a long and eventful history live on as an office building, perhaps even as the home of a managing director who then comes here a few times a year to supervise a trade fair? Of course, you have to be flexible as a building, but I agree with my residents that we would not like such a solution. We would all be delighted if a family with children were to move into my old walls. Then there will be a big renovation, I will be cleared out, rebuilt and refurnished. The traces of an eventful era of my life will be removed. But a new era will begin, and new life will come into my walls. My new residents will laugh and cry again, love and argue, eat and sleep, mourn and celebrate. Life goes on.

A Quick Decision

The house was right: life went on - and so much more! After all the thoughts, doubts and concerns, Cecilia and I realized that there was no point in weighing up all the eventualities again and again and losing a lot of time in the process. Everything had been discussed at length and very controversially among family and friends. Plan B was discussed from January 2022, and we made our decision at the end of March: Plan B became Plan A, for immediate implementation. We drew the Philippine card with all the consequences. That was the starting signal for what was probably the biggest project and adventure of our lives. This at the proud age of 74 and 78!

There were actually four projects that had to be tackled separately and sometimes simultaneously:

1. Clearing out the old house, selecting the inventory, packing and shipping that inventory to be taken to the Philippines;
2. Selling the old house;
3. Selecting and buying land, planning and building the new house;
4. Furnishing the new house and moving in.

So, we rolled up our sleeves and got to work. I drew a first rough sketch of how I imagined the bungalow for our 4-person senior community. A U-shaped building, with private rooms to the left and right and a shared living room, kitchen, dining room and large terrace in the middle. Our private area was to include a bedroom with a bathroom, a separate living room, a guest room and an office for me. I sent the design to Dante, our future construction manager and chief engineer. Cecilia began with an initial inspection of the household goods and preliminary discussions with her Filipino logistics expert Jerry, who had already regularly transported large parcels to her family for her. The two of them were already an experienced team. At this point, we already suspected that this was just the beginning and that it wouldn't be that easy.

Cecilia then traveled to the Philippines again for two weeks to kick things off there too.

Start of Construction

In the meantime, Cecilia's brother Israel had agreed to transfer a plot of land to us that had been offered to him. The plot belonged to the vice governor of the district, with whom Israel is friends. Cecilia, Dante and Nelia inspected the property and found it suitable. The decision was then made to build the house for our senior citizens' community on the plot together. At the same time, I transferred a large sum of money to Dante for the purchase of the plot and initial building work. Cecilia and the vice governor signed the contract, and the plot was purchased. The construction of our new house could begin.

The approximately 1,200 square meter plot is located in a suburb of Balanga City, the capital of the district of Bataan. A small road leads there from the highway about one kilometer away, from which a 100-metre-long cul-de-sac leads directly to our plot. The small peninsula of Bataan, which surrounds the bay of Manila, has two mountainous national parks that are only accessible to hikers. The highest mountains are 1,400 meters high, which is not at all low for a peninsula that is just over 20 kilometers wide. The mountains are correspondingly steep and beautiful to look at with their dense, evergreen forest. Balanga City is located on the east coast of the peninsula, where there are no beautiful beaches to be found. There are, however, half an hour's drive away on the west coast of the peninsula towards the South China Sea. Beaches, mountains, nature parks, everything in proximity - I never thought I would be able to choose a place like this to live. It seemed almost unreal to me, but now I knew it was going to happen.

Dante had already drawn up complete building plans with the plot details and submitted them. The inspection and approval process was surprisingly quick, probably also due to the prominent connections. As a result, Dante and his 14-man construction team were able to arrive and start work at the beginning of April. A well-coordinated and experienced team that had already built 9 smaller houses. Our new house was now to be their masterpiece.

The first step here is always to build a fence to secure the building materials delivered. In the Philippines, the fence is usually a two- to three-meter-high wall. For a German garden owner, that takes some getting used to. Then came the first big problem. The plot turned out to be a wetland, caused by water flowing down from the mountains during heavy rain. To keep the water out, the wall had to go deep into the ground and be specially sealed. Digging the deep trenches into the muddy ground was hard work and took a lot of time. An excavator could only be used in some places. Most of the time, the men stood in the mud in their light flip-flops. They spent the night in very makeshift camps on the construction site to guard the materials and tools.

But we tried to make the men's hard work a little easier. Dante and Nelia provided them with food, which is not usual here. This was gladly accepted, as were higher wages, even if these were still incredibly low by German standards. Broken shoes or clothes were replaced. If necessary, medical care was provided immediately and sufficiently. Fortunately, there were no serious accidents during the entire construction period. The men themselves were - like many Filipinos - masters of improvisation. When a monitor lizard strayed onto the construction site, it only survived for a short time, ended up on the barbecue and significantly improved the evening meat ration. A second monitor lizard had the same fate a little later. Despite the hard work, the atmosphere on the construction site was excellent.

Breaking Up

Back home in Düsseldorf, we began to systematically dismantle our familiar surroundings. The beginning farewell felt like the conscious ending of a long-term relationship. Because that's exactly how it was, we had both developed a close and loving relationship with the house and our furnishings.

I contacted a real estate agent I had met at an event years ago, Marcus Krüll. At the time, the event was entitled "How to sell a house without an estate agent". It ended subtly with the realization that you do need an estate agent. The man convinced me. We quickly agreed on a target purchase price and how to proceed. But I had two conditions for the selection of candidates: they had to be likeable to me and it had to be a family with children. After everything I had experienced in the house myself, I imagined it to be a paradise for children and young people. At least that's what I wanted it to be.

Back in my home office, I was hit by the big pity. The full shelves and cupboards contained so many memories and the results of my thoughts and actions, my life's work so far, so to speak. Meters and meters of files of all kinds, documents from my two limited companies, books that were important to me, hundreds of my own articles, publications, statements and minutes from my various activities, all copies of my "Journal for Noise Abatement" and countless personal mementos of all kinds. A lot of thinking and writing took place here, problems were solved, and decisions made, countless private and business trips were planned and booked, maintenance and repairs to the house were organized, bills were paid, and phone calls were made all over the world. And money was earned here. The income from self-employment was an important additional source of income for us for many years, and after I left Schwarz Pharma it even became the sole source of income, including for our many trips. What could I take with me to the Philippines from all this evidence of my work? The realization came quickly: almost nothing, it just didn't make sense. At that moment, it became very clear to me that this phase of my life was now over.

I made my decision. My "Journal for Noise Abatement" was now to be an example of all these treasures of memory! I was the sole editor responsible for this journal published by Springer, which I used to finance my medical studies, among other things. My job was to procure good specialist articles and get them ready for print. This was not always easy and required good and constant contact with potential authors. I wrote a summary of each article myself in German, English and French. There was no support from translation programs at the time. The magazine was published monthly, so the five volumes in my cupboard contained 60 copies in three piles. I took a deep breath and the first stack landed in a box. The next two followed immediately. The box was labeled WASTE PAPER in capital letters. I sat down at my desk and let the tears run free for a while. Then it was done. I could move on.

Wrapping Up

Cecilia has always been a wrapping artist. Every year for decades, she sent several large overseas boxes filled to the brim with clothes, household goods and long-life food to her family in the Philippines. They all reached their destination intact. Cecilia had a special method of making the boxes extremely sturdy and seaworthy: she wrapped the already strong cardboard completely with wide tape. The next step was to prepare ten boxes in this way and then fill them. Little did she know that she would end up with 40 of these large boxes.

That alone was time-consuming and involved a lot of physical work. But the real challenge was sorting all the household goods and packing them in a stable and break-proof way. Every time Cecilia had packed a box tightly and tightly, I was called in to close the box once and for all. But where to put the rest of the things? It was easiest in the cellar. Hazardous waste, glass, wood, metal and plastics went to the recycling center in almost daily trips in my fully loaded car. Larger items had to be carried up the narrow basement stairs to the driveway for the bulky waste. Sometimes friends helped with the hauling. A large cupboard had to be axed to fit through the cellar door. How did they get it into the cellar back then, we wondered helplessly.

We wanted to take some of our old furniture, all family heirlooms, with us. They were picked up by our Filipino logistician Jerry and packed separately. The other antique pieces and the fine wall unit found recipients among family and friends. Just as well, because selling the furniture proved to be difficult and not very lucrative. So, we gave away most of the remaining furniture and carpets via the local community "nebenan.de". That made for several happy faces. A Russian came with his toolbox to dismantle our bed. Unfortunately, the Allen key he needed was missing. Fortunately, I was able to borrow one from a neighbor. Overjoyed, the Russian spontaneously gave me a kiss on the cheek - my first Russian kiss. A Turk managed to transport our large corner sofa home from the living room on his small car. The police didn't see it or looked the other way. The house got emptier and emptier.

The most difficult part was the contents of the cupboards, chests of drawers and shelves. It was unbelievable what was hidden there! In addition to useful household items, there were also many things that hadn't been looked at or used for a long time but had a high sentimental value. These were gifts or souvenirs from trips, for example, some of which were really valuable. This initially left us a little perplexed, but we found an elegant solution: a mini flea market was set up next to the checkroom and advertised in "nebenan.de". Interested parties could register and then rummage through our forgotten treasures. Many a valuable item went over the table for a few euros, much to the delight of the buyers. In the end, everything that was somehow still usable was sold.

I've always told you that you should clean out the cellar and your cupboards thoroughly! Everything could have been sorted and distributed calmly and carefully in the past. Now, in the hectic rush of preparing for the move, everything just had to go as quickly as possible. But nobody listened to me. So now I've given away valuable old pocket watches and lots of other things for a few euros, and that's what you get for it!

In the meantime, the estate agent had done a great job. A high-quality exposé had been created that made my old house look like a stately mansion. The exposé had the somewhat grandiose title "Very well-maintained detached house in red brick construction with a flower-filled garden dream". A photographer was brought in especially for this purpose, who staged the house and garden from all sides, inside and out. The result impressed more than just us. The first prospective buyers soon came forward.

Who will Take Over my Old House?

We have rarely had so many visitors in such a short space of time. We set viewing days, usually at the weekends, on which the estate agent arranged appointments, mostly 4 per day. His employee then met the interested parties on the street in front of the house.

In total, around 20 interested parties came, often whole families. If the estate agent wasn't there yet or was still busy with the previous group, people stood at the front fence, looked curiously at the old brick walls and the tidy front garden and tried to process their first impressions.

Most of our many visitors were quite personable and seemed genuinely interested. The estate agent then showed them around the house according to a pre-arranged plan. She started in the spacious hallway with the old fireplace. All the doors were open, and the first view from there was into the living room and through the large windowpanes of the patio door into the well-tended garden. "First impressions are crucial," said the experienced estate agent, and the conversations that followed proved him right. Many of the visitors had already fallen in love with the old house at that moment. Once on the second floor, the visitors first met Cecilia and then me in my office. People got to know each other, conversations developed and quite a few visitors spontaneously took a liking to us. Cecilia always quickly made contact with the children who came along. One little girl was so impressed that she didn't want to let go of her new friend. Gummy bears probably also played a part in this. A visitor saw my literature about South America and confessed her enthusiasm for this continent. We talked for a while, and I spontaneously gave her my book "Encounters in Perú". Later, she also received the other books and illustrated books, as I didn't want to take them with me to the Philippines. And then there were tears. Two families liked the house so much that they wanted to have it immediately. And we really liked both families. After 5 days of viewings and the first concrete negotiations, we had had enough of the many visitors and stopped further viewings. In our hearts, we had already made up our minds.

Why doesn't anyone ask how I fared during these visits? First, I was cleaned and made up, then I was asked to pose as a model for a photographer. And then all these people came and looked in all my corners and asked about my weak points. And I was always supposed to show my best side. Admittedly, the exposé flattered me, "very well-kept, flowery, garden dream", you don't hear that every day. And the photos were also very flattering, I didn't even know beforehand just how many of my best sides I had. And then there were so many compliments during the visits, people even cried. To be honest: I actually enjoyed being the center of attention! The only remaining question is who will take me on. I'm glad that my landlord has opted for a family and that I won't become an office building. My landlord's mostly untidy office is more than enough for me. I want a lot of young life within my old walls!

Although we already had a clear favorite, three parties were shortlisted. Then the estate agent started the actual negotiations. One of the last two families quickly left because the financing seemed hopeless. The family, who were enthusiastic about South America, had two older children who no longer lived at home. However, they were prepared to pay the full price. And our favorite, the family with two teenage daughters, also struggled with the price and financing. But our decision was quickly made. We followed our hearts and came a long way towards our favorites with the price, right down to the pain threshold. They were awarded the contract. The handover was agreed for September 1.

Now the whole thing had to be notarized. A routine process, but there were pitfalls here too: the notary discovered that there were still charges entered in the land register. In fact, I had registered the house as security for two loans, one for major repairs and the other for the purchase of our medical practice. Both loans had long since been repaid but had not been deleted from the land register. Fortunately, my bank was cooperative and was able to quickly provide the relevant documents from previous years. Nothing stood in the way of the notary appointment.

The New Homeowners

We didn't have to look far to find the friendly young family we wanted to take over my old house. Slobodan ("Bo") and Milena with their two daughters Paula and Anna and dog Vito were exactly the family we had wanted and imagined. And the house was obviously love at first sight for them too. Milena had tears in her eyes during the first viewing when she discovered the old, tiled stove and Vito exploring the well-tended garden for the first time as his possible future territory. Bo, an experienced kitchen remodeling expert, already had new room designs in mind during the first viewing. A bit of a shock for us: our living room, which we called the "lobby" because we only used it when we had guests, was to become the new kitchen. And a big shock for Milena: the tiled stove no longer had a place in this plan. We discreetly withdrew from this topic. Because even Cecilia had to swallow hard at the thought of the beautiful stove disappearing. But the obvious joy of seeing the young family and being part of their big plans made the growing pain of separation more bearable. Because with the notary appointment coming up, it was official that it would soon no longer be my house.

On the day of the appointment, we met with the couple in the notary's elegant waiting room. We were served a chilled fruit juice with a view overlooking the Königsallee. By now we had grown fond of Bo and Milena. Despite the big business, we felt much more like friends than business partners. So, it was rather cheerful entering the conference room, where the notary began to read out the extensive contract after a brief greeting. We had all read it beforehand, so I was probably not the only one struggling with fatigue during the monotonous reading. The contract was sealed with a series of signatures. My old house was no longer mine.

Now I needed a big glass of wine. It was still afternoon, a beautiful, warm summer's day. We invited our new friends to dinner at the Fischhaus in the nearby old town. It wasn't very busy at this time of day, so we got a table on the lovely shady terrace by the street. The tension of the official ceremony quickly evaporated in the relaxed atmosphere of the old town. We talked a lot and got to know each other better - a wonderful end to this important day for all of us.

Our New House is Being Built

It took several months until the boundary walls were finally in place and kept the water out of the ground. Then the pool and cellar were dug out and the rest of the site was filled in, raising it considerably. The wetland had become a dry and buildable base for our new house. The hard work had paid off. And the rainwater collected in the pool pit and provided some welcome refreshment after the work was done. A well was also drilled for their own water supply. Basements are a rarity in the Philippines, but we at least wanted to build a basement for the kitchen to have more space for storage and supplies. Speaking of the kitchen: Dante had revised my rough planning sketch in detail and redesigned everything apart from our private area. One of the results was a huge kitchen with an impressive 60 square meters of floor space. As a result, the basement was also brought up to the same size and therefore offered much more space than originally planned. The spacious kitchen was mainly at the expense of Dante and Nelia's private rooms, which were correspondingly more modest. This was intentional, as the kitchen is probably the most important living space and meeting place for the family in the Philippines. This is where meals are served, and guests are received. The rarely used living room is more for official and representative occasions.

The first walls were built for the staff house. Once roofed, it finally offered the construction team stable and dry accommodation. The walls of the residential building went up surprisingly quickly. In the meantime, the construction team had grown to 27 men by the help of local workers. The roof of the house proved to be more difficult. Placing the heavy metal parts on the rather large bungalow required physically demanding and precise work. Then a typhoon hit the country, causing a further delay of two weeks. But finally, the roof was finished, and the interior work could begin.

A Move with Detours

After we left our old house, we were "homeless" for a while and went on a short round trip to visit a few places near to the rivers Rhine, Nahe and Moselle that we had fond memories of. In mid-September, Cecilia wanted to fly to the Philippines for good, while I planned to continue my tour of Germany for a while longer. Shortly before departure, however, she was caught by the coronavirus. Fortunately, she was feeling better again on the day of departure. I took her to Amsterdam airport with her 70 kg luggage. In the meantime, she had also infected me, and I was feeling really bad. So, I dropped her off at check-in and then immediately went to bed in an airport hotel for a few days. My round trip then took me through the Netherlands to friends in northern Germany, Münsterland and the Rhineland and finally to the Black Forest, where I went on a hike to a viewpoint. On the way back, a shortcut proved to be my undoing. I jumped down a small rock step, slipped on the wet rocky ground, hit the ground and rolled sideways down a few more meters. It took me a while to get back up and find my glasses again. It was the long weekend around October 3rd, and I didn't want to use the weekend service of a "Black Forest clinic". Somehow, I made it to Düsseldorf by car in several stages, but it was hell. There, a trauma surgeon friend told me the diagnosis: 6 broken ribs. It wasn't until October 12, after a few painful days in the Hotel, that I was able to follow Cecilia to the Philippines, also with a lot of luggage, which gave me with my broken ribs still a lot of problems to solve.

In the meantime, the new building had progressed further: The basement ceiling, electricity and water installations, drainage, plastering walls, pulling in ceilings and laying floors, there was progress everywhere. Bit by bit, it became clear what the rooms would look like in the future. It was a wonderful and exciting time that we spent together with Nelia and Dante in two very modest apartments near the construction site. Finally, the last design elements, fittings, tiles, wall paints and lamps were added.

A few weeks before the final work, when all 27 men were still on site, we wanted to express our satisfaction and gratitude. A party was organized, there was lots of delicious food, I had prepared a speech and 27 envelopes with a tidy bonus were ready. Shortly before the buffet opened, I gave my speech and received friendly nods and polite applause. Only - as I found out later - hardly anyone had understood my English words! My assumption that everyone spoke English because it is the official language proved to be an illusion. Worse still, many thought the money Cecilia handed over was a final payment and the speech was a dismissal. As a result, some of the local workers didn't show up for work the next day. Dante and his foreman had to pick them up one by one. Saving face is an Asian virtue, so it's better to nod and applaud than admit you didn't understand, and don't expect me to be confronted with my rhetorical failure either.

After all, moving into our new home was our Christmas present. On December 24, 2022, we left the small apartments and moved into our new space. That evening, we took the time to enjoy our first Christmas in our new home. However, 40 overseas boxes and some furniture and pictures that were still packed were waiting for us there. They would keep us busy for a few more weeks and months. Once again, we rolled up our sleeves.

Old Walls in a New Outfit

The new owners left nothing to chance. Even before the handover, they had asked for another inspection. And so, on a Saturday morning, 10 craftsmen from various disciplines arrived at the same time to carry out a thorough inspection of the house with a view to planned renovation work. Naturally, Bo and Milena wanted to know what was possible and what the costs would be. They spent several hours measuring, drawing, discussing and taking notes. Then calm returned and we were able to continue with the final clean-up work.

The handover of the house on August 31 was then just a formal act, but nevertheless very friendly and emotional. The meter readings were taken and photographed in the presence of the estate agent, and the keys were placed neatly on a bench. The new owners' anticipation and impatience for the upcoming renovation was clearly palpable. A photo with the old and new owners in front of the front door marked the end. It was done, this part of our big plan was complete.

The very next day, they started taking me apart. Even as the many workmen were carrying out their inspections, I felt like a patient in hospital before an operation. And so it was, the operation began in many places at once, for example with the painful ripping off the wallpaper. My old landlord had always used extra strong wallpaper paste and said: "What I have glued together, let no man put asunder". Unfortunately, this proved to be true, as the old, somewhat crumbling plaster often came down with the wallpaper. A piece of ceiling also broke down, revealing water damage that had probably been caused by a leak in the roof years ago. The passageway between the living room and dining room, which Schufti had laboriously broken out at the time, was widened to two meters, not without first pulling in the steel beams needed to support it. The old, tiled stove fell victim to the conversion, as it had not been in use for decades anyway. The kitchen and bathroom were gutted, the kitchen was turned into a guest room and the old living room was converted into a kitchen. My ground floor and first floor were given new parquet flooring. The entire electrical installation, which was admittedly quite dilapidated, was replaced, as was the 25-year-old heating system. External blinds soon ensured a better indoor climate.

The most spectacular conversion took place on the second floor. The unused large attic and two small rooms were to become a paradise for Paula and Anna. Just a few days after the handover, five new skylights adorned my old roof and provided plenty of light in the paradise that was being created. In between, the entire roof was effectively insulated. The cladding in the rooms was renewed, revealing a lot of rubble that had been disposed of behind the walls. The passageway between the rooms was closed. The large open loft was turned into a shared living room for the two girls. The highlight, however, is the bathroom with its own window, which was newly installed on the second floor. My draughty attic and the two rooms that had always remained provisional were turned into a chic teenage apartment.

The entire renovation took over three months. The family struggled to achieve their ambitious goal of moving in on December 1. But they made it, even if a few adjustments were necessary afterwards. A regular daily routine returned to my walls, which shone with new splendor and modern design.

Mission Completed!

Just in time for the start of 2023, our major project was by and large successfully completed. We have built a new home for ourselves in Bataan in the Philippines, where we feel comfortable in the comunity with Nelia and Dante and, embedded in Cecilia's large family, somehow also feel safe. We enjoy the beautiful surroundings and the mostly very pleasant climate. Exploring the area always leads us to new beautiful destinations. Longer tours, for example to the rice terraces in the mountains, to the Taal volcano or to other islands, have also been on the program. In the meantime, we have established ourselves here and have already made some new friends. And I now also have a Philippine pensioner's identity card, which I now accept and use actively. Occasional visits to my old home and constant contact via social media make the separation and homesickness bearable. And what is no less important to me is that we have also taken good care of my old house. A picture-perfect family has moved in and is filling the old house with new life. It didn't take long for us to receive the first pictures of happy celebrations on the old terrace.

I think we can be proud of the quick and successful implementation of our project. It took just less than a year from the creation of a Plan B (Philippines) instead of the retirement home on offer in January 2022 to the finished new home. This would not have been possible without a lot of external support: The perfect organization of the house sale by our estate agent Marcus Krüll, the equally perfect handling of the move by our logistician Jerry, important contacts with local authorities by Cecilia's brother Israel and, last but not least, the tireless efforts of Nelia and Dante in the planning and construction of the new house. But we also paid our price. Significant emotional and physical stress made 2022 a very difficult year for us. Our COVID-19 illnesses and my bad fall with broken ribs made things even more difficult. In the end, we were both exhausted and needed a longer period of time in our new environment to recover to some extent. After all, we were already 74 and 78 years old in that difficult year, fortunately in reasonably good health. We can only advise anyone planning a similar project: Do it 10 years earlier!

I am also very happy with the new situation! Fortunately, my fear that I would degenerate into an office building, commercial apartment or rental property was unfounded. On the contrary, my old landlord's vision has been fulfilled: A young family has converted me according to their wishes and ideas and some necessities, feels at home within my old walls and brings in a lot of new joie de vivre. There was a lot of talk of love in this story. Even a house wants to be loved. In this respect, I've never been able to complain, and I'm not complaining now either. My builder, the late Aunt Luise, would be pleased with me. A new era has begun for me, and I have the certain feeling that it will be another good time. A heartfelt thank you and a farewell to the Philippines!

Dear house, thank you, it was wonderful with you! After all, I have spent a large part of my life within your walls and Cecilia a good 35 years. It is important to me, and I am very happy that you are doing well! Above all, I wish you, your residents and all of us that you never have to experience wartime again.
So long, old house, good luck!